PERSONALITY

"'What is this anyway? A George Cohan comedy?'"—*Page 153*

PERSONALITY PLUS

Some Experiences of Emma McChesney
and Her Son, Jock

Edna Ferber

Illustrated by
James Montgomery Flagg

University of Illinois Press
Urbana and Chicago

First Illinois paperback, 2002
Manufactured in the United States of America
P 5 4 3 2 1

♾ This book is printed on acid-free paper.

Library of Congress Cataloging-in-Publication Data
Ferber, Edna, 1887-1968.
Personality plus : some experiences of Emma
McChesney and her son, Jock / Edna Ferber ;
illustrated by James Montgomery Flagg.
        p. cm.
ISBN 0-252-07087-9 (paper : alk. paper)
1. McChesney, Emma (Fictitious character)—
Fiction. 2. Traveling sales personnel—Fiction.
3. Women sales personnel—Fiction. 4. Mothers and
sons—Fiction. 5. Businesswomen—Fiction.
6. Adventure stories, American. 7. Domestic fiction,
American. I. Title.
        PS3511.E46P47   2002
        813'.52—dc21   002017129

CONTENTS

ILLUSTRATIONS

PERSONALITY PLUS

PERSONALITY PLUS

I

MAKING GOOD WITH MOTHER

WHEN men began to build cities vertically instead of horizontally there passed from our highways a picturesque figure, and from our language an expressive figure of speech. That oily-tongued, persuasive, soft-stepping stranger in the rusty Prince Albert and the black string tie who had been wont to haunt our back steps and front offices with his carefully wrapped bundle, retreated in bewildered defeat before the clanging blows of steel on steel that meant the erection of the first twenty-story skyscraper. "As slick," we used to say, "as a lightning-rod agent." Of what use his wares on a building whose tower was robed in clouds and which used the chain lightning for a necklace? The Fourth Avenue antique dealer had another curio to add to his collection of andirons, knockers, snuff boxes and warming pans.

But even as this quaint figure vanished there sprang up a new and glittering one to take his place. He stood framed in the great plate-glass window of the very building which had brought about the defeat of his predecessor. A miracle of close shaving his face was, and a marvel of immaculateness his linen. Dapper he was, and dressy, albeit inclined to glittering effects and a certain plethory at the back of the neck. Back of him stood shining shapes that reflected his glory in enamel, and brass, and glass. His language was floral, but choice; his talk was of gearings and bearings and cylinders and magnetos; his method differed from that of him who went before as the method of a skilled aëronaut differs from that of the man who goes over Niagara in a barrel. And as he multiplied and spead over the land we coined a new figure of speech. " Smooth! " we chuckled. " As smooth as an automobile salesman."

But even as we listened, fascinated by his fluent verbiage there grew within us a certain resentment. Familiarity with his glittering wares bred a contempt of them, so that he fell to speaking of them as necessities instead of luxuries. He juggled figures, and thought nothing of four of them in a row. We looked at our five-thousand-dollar salary, so strangely shrunken and thin now, and even as we looked we saw that the method of the unctuous, anxious stranger had become antiquated in its turn.

Then from his ashes emerged a new being. Neither urger nor spellbinder he. The twentieth century was stamped across his brow, and on his lips was ever the word " Service." Silent, courteous, watchful, alert, he listened, while you talked. His method, in turn, made that of the silk-lined salesman sound like the hoarse hoots of the ballyhoo man at a county fair. Blithely he accepted five hundred thousand dollars and gave in return — a promise. And when we would search our soul for a synonym to express all that was low-voiced, and suave, and judicious, and patient, and sure, we began to say, " As alert as an advertising expert."

Jock McChesney, looking as fresh and clear-eyed as only twenty-one and a cold shower can make one look, stood in the doorway of his mother's bedroom. His toilette had halted abruptly at the bathrobe stage. One of those bulky garments swathed his slim figure, while over his left arm hung a gray tweed Norfolk coat. From his right hand dangled a pair of trousers, in pattern a modish black-and-white.

Jock regarded the gray garment on his arm with moody eyes.

" Well, I'd like to know what's the matter with it! " he demanded, a trifle irritably.

Emma McChesney, in the act of surveying her back hair in the mirror, paused, hand glass poised half way, to regard her son.

" All right," she answered cheerfully. " I'll tell you. It's too young."

" Young! " He held it at arm's length and stared at it. " What d'you mean — young? "

Emma McChesney came forward, wrapping the folds of her kimono about her. She took the disputed garment in one hand and held it aloft. " I know that you look like a man on a magazine cover in it. But Norfolk suits spell tennis, and seashore, and elegant leisure. And you're going out this morning, Son, to interview business men. You're going to try to impress the advertising world with the fact that it needs your expert services. You walk into a business office in a Norfolk suit, and everybody from the office boy to the president of the company will ask you what your score is."

She tossed it back over his arm.

"I'll wear the black and white," said Jock resignedly, and turned toward his own room. At his doorway he paused and raised his voice slightly: "For that matter, they're looking for young men. Everybody's young. Why, the biggest men in the advertising game are just kids." He disappeared within his room, still talking. "Look at McQuirk, advertising manager of the Combs Car Company. He's so young he has to disguise himself in bone-trimmed eye-glasses with a black ribbon to get away with it. Look at Hopper, of the Berg, Shriner Company. Pulls down ninety thousand a year, and if he's thirty-five I'll —"

"Well, you asked my advice," interrupted his mother's voice with that muffled effect which is caused by a skirt being slipped over the head, "and I gave it. Wear a white duck sailor suit with blue anchors and carry a red tin pail and a shovel, if you want to look young. Only get into it in a jiffy, Son, because breakfast will be

ready in ten minutes. I can tell by the way
Annie's crashing the cups. So step lively if
you want to pay your lovely mother's subway
fare."

Ten minutes later the slim young figure, in
its English-fitting black and white, sat opposite
Emma McChesney at the breakfast table and
between excited gulps of coffee outlined a mete-
oric career in his chosen field. And the more
he talked and the rosier his figures of speech became, the more silent and thoughtful fell his
mother. She wondered if five o'clock would
find a droop to the set of those young shoulders;
if the springy young legs in their absurdly scant
modish trousers would have lost some of their
elasticity; if the buoyant step in the flat-heeled
shoes would not drag a little. Thirteen years
of business experience had taught her to swal-
low smilingly the bitter pill of rebuff. But this
boy was to experience his first dose to-day.
She felt again that sensation of almost physical
nausea — that sickness of heart and spirit
which had come over her when she had met her
first sneer and intolerant shrug. It had been
her maiden trip on the road for the T. A. Buck
Featherloom Petticoat Company. She was

secretary of that company now, and moving spirit in its policy. But the wound of that first insult still ached. A word from her would have placed the boy and saved him from curt refusals. She withheld that word. He must fight his fight alone.

" I want to write the kind of ad," Jock was saying excitedly, " that you see 'em staring at in the subways, and street cars and L-trains. I want to sit across the aisle and watch their up-turned faces staring at that oblong, and reading it aloud to each other."

" Isn't that an awfully obvious necktie you're wearing, Jock?" inquired his mother irrele-vantly.

" This? You ought to see some of them. This is a Quaker stock in comparison." He glanced down complacently at the vivid-hued silken scarf that the season's mode demanded. Immediately he was off again. " And the first thing you know, Mrs. McChesney, ma'am, we'll have a motor truck backing up at the door once a month and six strong men carrying my salary to the freight elevator in sacks."

Emma McChesney buttered her bit of toast, then looked up to remark quietly:

[7]

"Hadn't you better qualify for the trial heats, Jock, before you jump into the finals?"

"Trial heats!" sneered Jock. "They're poky. I want real money. Now! It isn't enough to be just well-to-do in these days. It needs money. I want to be rich! Not just prosperous, but rich! So rich that I can let the bath soap float around in the water without any pricks of conscience. So successful that they'll say, 'And he's a mere boy, too. Imagine!'"

And, "Jock dear," Emma McChesney said, "you've still to learn that plans and ambitions are like soap bubbles. The harder you blow and the more you inflate them, the quicker they burst. Plans and ambitions are things to be kept locked away in your heart, Son, with no one but yourself to take an occasional peep at them."

Jock leaned over the table, with his charming smile. "You're a jealous blonde," he laughed. "Because I'm going to be a captain of finance — an advertising wizard; you're afraid I'll grab the glory all away from you."

Mrs. McChesney folded her napkin and rose. She looked unbelievably young, and

"You're a jealous blond," he said"—*Page 8*

trim, and radiant, to be the mother of this boasting boy.

" I'm not afraid," she drawled, a wicked little glint in her blue eyes. " You see, they'll only regard your feats and say, ' H'm, no wonder. He ought to be able to sell ice to an Eskimo. His mother was Emma McChesney.' "

And then, being a modern mother, she donned smart autumn hat and tailored suit coat and stood ready to reach her office by nine-thirty. But because she was as motherly as she was modern she swung open the door between kitchen and dining-room to advise with Annie, the adept.

" Lamb chops to-night, eh, Annie? And sweet potatoes. Jock loves 'em. And corn au gratin and some head lettuce." She glanced toward Jock in the hallway, then lowered her voice. " Annie," she teased, " just give us one of your peach cobblers, will you? You see he — he's going to be awfully — tired when he gets home."

So they went stepping off to work together, mother and son. A mother of twenty-five years before would have watched her son with tear-dimmed eyes from the vine-wreathed porch of a cottage. There was no watching a son from the tenth floor of an up-town apartment house. Besides, she had her work to do. The subway swallowed both of them. Together they jostled and swung their way down-town in the close packed train. At the Twenty-third Street station Jock left her.

" You'll have dinner to-night with a full-fledged professional gent," he bragged, in his youth and exuberance and was off down the aisle and out on the platform. Emma Mc-Chesney managed to turn in her nine-inch space of train seat so that she watched the slim, buoyant young figure from the window until the train drew away and he was lost in the stairway jam. Just so Rachel had watched the boy Joseph go to meet the Persian caravans in the desert.

" Don't let them buffalo you, Jock," Emma had said, just before he left her. " They'll try it. If they give you a broom and tell you to sweep down the back stairs, take it, and sweep, and don't forget the corners. And if, while you're sweeping, you notice that that kind of broom isn't suited to the stairs go in and suggest a new kind. They'll like it."

Brooms and back stairways had no place in Jock McChesney's mind as the mahogany and gold elevator shot him up to the fourteenth floor of the great office building that housed the Berg, Shriner Company. Down the marble hallway he went and into the reception room. A cruel test it was, that reception room, with the cruelty peculiar to the modern in business. With its soft-shaded lamp, its two-toned rug, its Jacobean chairs, its magazine-laden cathedral oak table, its pot of bright flowers making a smart touch of color in the somber richness of the room, it was no place for the shabby, the down-and-out, the cringing, the rusty, or the mendicant.

Jock McChesney, from the tips of his twelve-dollar shoes to his radiant face, took the test and stood it triumphantly. He had entered with an air in which was mingled the briskness of assurance with the languor of ease. There were times when Jock McChesney was every inch the son of his mother.

There advanced toward Jock a large, plump, dignified personage, a personage courteous, yet reserved, inquiring, yet not offensively curious — a very Machiavelli of reception-room ushers. Even while his lips questioned, his eyes appraised clothes, character, conduct.

"Mr. Hupp, please," said Jock, serene in the perfection of his shirt, tie, collar and scarf pin, upon which the appraising eye now rested. "Mr. McChesney." He produced a card.

"Appointment?"

"No — but he'll see me."

But Machiavelli had seen too many overconfident callers. Their very confidence had taught him caution.

"If you will please state your — ah — business —"

Jock smiled a little patient smile and brushed an imaginary fleck of dust from the sleeve of his very correct coat.

"I want to ask him for a job as office boy," he jibed.

An answering grin overspread the fat features of the usher. Even an usher likes his little joke. The sense of humor dies hard.

"I have a letter from him, asking me to call," said Jock, to clinch it.

"This way." The keeper of the door led

Jock toward the sacred inner portal and held it open. " Mr. Hupp's is the last door to the right."

The door closed behind him. Jock found himself in the big, busy, light-flooded central office. Down either side of the great room ran a row of tiny private offices, each partitioned off, each outfitted with desk, and chairs, and a big, bright window. On his way to the last door at the right Jock glanced into each tiny office, glimpsing busy men bent absorbedly over papers, girls busy with dictation, here and there a door revealing two men, or three, deep in discussion of a problem, heads close together, voices low, faces earnest. It came suddenly to the smartly modish, overconfident boy walking the length of the long room that the last person needed in this marvelously perfected and smooth-running organization was a somewhat awed young man named Jock McChesney. There came to him that strange sensation which comes to every job-hunter; that feeling of having his spiritual legs carry him out of the room, past the door, down the hall and into the street, even as, in reality, they bore him on to the very presence which he dreaded and yet wished to see.

Two steps more, and he stood in the last doorway, right. No matinée idol, nervously awaiting his cue in the wings, could have planned his entrance more carefully than Jock had planned this. Ease was the thing; ease, bordering on nonchalance, mixed with a brisk and businesslike assurance.

The entrance was lost on the man at the desk. He did not even look up. If Jock had entered on all-fours, doing a double tango to vocal accompaniment, it is doubtful if the man at the desk would have looked up. Pencil between his fingers, head held a trifle to one side in critical contemplation of the work before him, eyes narrowed judicially, lips pursed, he was the concentrated essence of do-it-now.

Jock waited a moment, in silence. The man at the desk worked on. His head was semi-bald. Jock knew him to be thirty. Jock fixed his eye on the semi-bald spot and spoke.

" My name's McChesney," he began. " I wrote you three days ago; you probably will remember. You replied, asking me to call, and I —"

" Minute," exploded the man at the desk, still absorbed.

[14]

"He was the concentrated essence of
do-it-now "— *Page 14*

Jock faltered, stopped. The man at the desk did not look up. A moment of silence, except for the sound of the busy pencil traveling across the paper. Jock, glaring at the semi-bald spot, spoke again.

" Of course, Mr. Hupp, if you're too busy to see me —"

" M-m-m-m," a preoccupied hum, such as a busy man makes when he is trying to give attention to two interests.

"— why I suppose there's no sense in staying; but it seems to me that common courtesy —"

The busy pencil paused, quivered in the making of a final period, enclosed the dot in a proof-reader's circle, and rolled away across the desk, its work done.

" Now," said Sam Hupp, and swung around, smiling, to face the affronted Jock. " I had to get that out. They're waiting for it." He pressed a desk button. " What can I do for you? Sit down, sit down."

There was a certain abrupt geniality about him. His tortoise-rimmed glasses gave him an oddly owlish look, like a small boy taking liberties with grandfather's spectacles.

[17]

Jock found himself sitting down, his anger slipping from him.

" My name's McChesney," he began. " I'm here because I want to work for this concern." He braced himself to present the convincing, reason-why arguments with which he had prepared himself.

Whereupon Sam Hupp, the brisk, proceeded to whisk his breath and arguments away with an unexpected:

" All right. What do you want to do? "

Jock's mouth fell open. " Do! " he stammered. " Do! Why — anything —"

Sam Hupp's quick eye swept over the slim, attractive, radiant, correctly-garbed young figure before him. Unconsciously he rubbed his bald spot with a rueful hand.

" Know anything about writing, or advertising? "

Jock was at ease immediately. " Quite a lot; yes. I practically rewrote the Gridiron play that we gave last year, and I was assistant advertising manager of the college publications for two years. That gives a fellow a pretty broad knowledge of advertising."

" Oh, Lord! " groaned Sam Hupp, and covered his eyes with his hand, as if in pain.

Jock stared. The affronted feeling was returning. Sam Hupp recovered himself and smiled a little wistfully.

" McChesney, when I came up here twelve years ago I got a job as reception-room usher. A reception-room usher is an office boy in long pants. Sometimes, when I'm optimistic, I think that if I live twelve years longer I'll begin to know something about the rudiments of this game."

" Oh, of course," began Jock, apologetically. But Hupp's glance was over his head. Involuntarily Jock turned to follow the direction of his eyes.

" Busy? " said a voice from the doorway.

" Come in, Dutch! Come in! " boomed Hupp.

The man who entered was of the sort that the boldest might well hesitate to address as " Dutch "— a tall, slim, elegant figure, Vandyked, bronzed.

" McChesney, this is Von Herman, head of our art department."

Their hands met in a brief clasp. Von Herman's thoughts were evidently elsewhere.

"Just wanted to tell you that that cussed model's skipped out. Gone with a show. Just when I had the whole series blocked out in my mind. He was a wonder. No brains, but a marvel for looks and style. These people want real stuff. Don't know how I'm going to give it to them now."

Hupp sat up. "Got to!" he snapped. "Campaign's late, as it is. Can't you get an ordinary man model and fake the Greek god beauty?"

"Yes — but it'll look faked. If I could lay my hands on a chap who could wear clothes as if they belonged to him —"

Hupp rose. "Here's your man," he cried, with a snap of his fingers. "Clothes! Look at him. He invented 'em. Why, you could photograph him and he'd look like a drawing."

Von Herman turned, surprised, incredulous, hopeful, his artist eye brightening at the ease and grace and modishness of the smart, well-knit figure before him.

[20]

"Me!" exploded Jock, his face suffused with a dull, painful red. "Me! Pose! For a clothing ad!"

"Well," Hupp reminded him, "you said you'd do anything."

Jock McChesney glared belligerently. Hupp returned the stare with a faint gleam of amusement shining behind the absurd glasses. The amused look changed to surprise as he beheld the glare in Jock's eyes fading. For even as he glared there had come a warning to Jock — a warning sent just in time from that wireless station located in his subconscious mind. A vivid face, full of pride, and hope, and encouragement flashed before him.

"Jock," it said, "don't let 'em buffalo you. They'll try it. If they give you a broom and tell you to sweep down the back stairs —"

Jock was smiling his charming, boyish smile.

"Lead me to your north light," he laughed at Von Herman. "Got any Robert W. Chambers's heroines tucked away there?"

Hupp's broad hand came down on his shoulder with a thwack. "That's the spirit, McChesney! That's the —" He stopped, abruptly. " Say, are you related to Mrs. Emma McChesney, of the Featherloom Skirt Company? "

" Slightly. She's my one and only mother."

" She — you mean — her son! Well I'll be darned! " He held out his hand to Jock. " If you're a real son of your mother I wish you'd just call the office boy as you step down the hall with Von Herman and tell him to bring me a hammer and a couple of spikes. I'd better nail down my desk."

" I'll promise not to crowd you for a year or two," grinned Jock from the doorway, and was off with the pleased Von Herman.

Past the double row of beehives again, into the elevator, out again, up a narrow iron stairway, into a busy, cluttered, skylighted room. Pictures, posters, photographs hung all about. Some of the pictures Jock recognized as old friends that had gazed familiarly at him from subway trains and street cars and theater programmes. Golf clubs, tennis rackets, walking sticks, billiard cues were stacked up in corners. And yet there was a bare and orderly look about the place. Two silent, shirt-sleeved men were busy at drawing boards. Through a doorway beyond Jock could see others similarly engaged in the next room. On a platform in one corner of the room posed a young man in one of those costumes the coat of which is a mongrel mixture of cutaway and sack. You see them worn by clergymen with unsecular ideas in dress, and by the leader of the counterfeiters' gang in the moving pictures. The pose was that met with in the backs of magazines — the head lifted, eyes fixed on an interesting object unseen, one arm crooked to hold a cane, one foot advanced, the other trailing slightly to give a Fifth Avenue four o'clock air. His face was expressionless. On his head was a sadly unironed silk hat.

Von Herman glanced at the drawing tacked to the board of one of the men. " That'll do, Flynn," he said to the model. He glanced again at the drawing. " Bring out the hat a little more, Mack. They won't burnish it if you don't,"— to the artist. Then, turning about, " Where's that girl? "

From a far corner, sheltered by long green curtains, stepped a graceful almost childishly slim figure in a bronze-green Norfolk suit and close-fitting hat from beneath which curled a

fluff of bright golden hair. Von Herman
stared at her.

"You're not the girl," he said. "You
won't do."

"You sent for me," retorted the girl. "I'm
Miss Michelin — Gelda Michelin. I posed
for you six months ago, but I've been out of
town with the show since then."

Von Herman, frowning, opened a table
drawer, pulled out a card index, ran his long
fingers through it and extracted a card. He
glanced at it, and then, the frown deepening,
read it aloud.

"'Michelin, Gelda. Telephone Bryant
4759. Brunette. Medium build. Good neck
and eyes. Good figure. Good clothes.'"

He glanced up. "Well?"

"That's me," said Miss Michelin calmly.
"I've got the same telephone number and eyes
and neck and clothes. Of course my hair is
different and I am thinner, but that's business.
I'd like to know what chance a fat girl would
have in the chorus these days."

Von Herman groaned. "I'll pay you for the
time you've waited and for your trouble. Can't
use you for these pictures." Then as she left

he turned a comically despairing face to the two men at the drawing boards. "What are we going to do? We've got to make a start on these pictures and everything has gone wrong. They want something special. Two figures, young man and woman. Said expressly they didn't want a chicken. No romping curls and none of that eyes and lips fool-girl stuff. This chap's ideal for the man." He pointed to Jock.

Jock had been staring, fascinated, at the shaded, zigzag marks which the artist — a dark-skinned, velvet-eyed, foreign-looking youth — was making on the sheet of paper before him. He had scarcely glanced up during the entire scene. Now he looked briefly and coolly at Jock.

"Where did you get him?" he asked, with the precise enunciation of the foreign-born. "Good figure. And he wears his clothes not like a cab driver, as the others do."

"Thanks," drawled Jock, flushing a little. Then, boyish curiosity getting the better of him, "Say, tell me, what in the world are you doing to that drawing?"

He of the velvety eyes smiled a twisted little

[25]

smile. His slim brown fingers never stopped in their work of guiding the pen in its zigzag path.

" It is work," he sneered, " to delight the soul of an artist. I am now engaged in the pleasing task of putting the bones in a herring-bone suit."

But Jock did not smile. Here was another man, he thought, who had been given a broom and told to sweep down the stairway.

Von Herman was regarding him almost wistfully. " I hate to let you slip," he said. Then, his face brightening, " By Jove! I wonder if Miss Galt would pose for us if we told her what a fix we were in."

He picked up the telephone receiver. " Miss Galt, please," he said. Then, aside, " Of course it's nerve to ask a girl who's earning three thousand a year to leave her desk and come up and pose for — Hello! Miss Galt?"

Jock, seated on the edge of the models' platform, was beginning to enjoy himself. Even this end of the advertising business had its interesting side, he thought. Ten minutes later he knew it had.

Ten minutes later there appeared Miss Galt. Jock left off swinging his legs from the platform and stood up. Miss Galt was that kind of girl. Smooth black hair parted and coiled low as only an exquisitely shaped head can dare to wear its glory-crown. A face whose expression was sweetly serious in spite of its youth. A girl whose clothes were the sort of clothes that girls ought to wear in offices, and don't.

" This is mighty good of you, Miss Galt," began Von Herman. " It's the Kool Komfort Klothes Company's summer campaign stuff. We'll only need you for an hour or so — to get the expression and general outline. Poster stuff, really. Then this young man will pose for the summer union suit pictures."

" Don't apologize," said Miss Galt. " We had a hard enough time to get that Kool Komfort account. We don't want to start wrong with the pictures. Besides, I think posing's real fun."

Jock thought so too, quite suddenly. Just as suddenly Von Herman remembered the conventions and introduced them.

" McChesney? " repeated Miss Galt, crisply.

[27]

" I know a Mrs. McChesney, of the T. A. Buck —"

" My mother," proudly.

" Your mother! Then why —" She stopped.

" Because," said Jock, " I'm the rawest rooky in the Berg, Shriner Company. And when I begin to realize what I don't know about advertising I'll probably want to plunge off the Palisades."

Miss Galt smiled up at him, her clear, frank eyes meeting his.

" You'll win," she said.

" Even if I lose — I win now," said Jock, suddenly audacious.

" Hi! Hold that pose! " called Von Herman, happily.

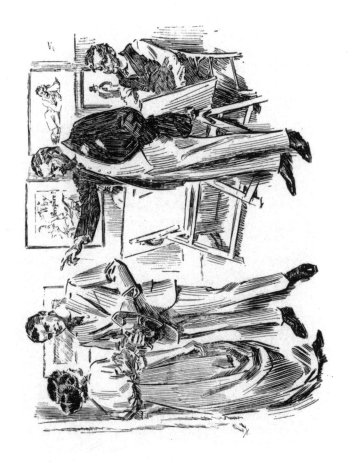

"'Hi! Hold that pose!' called Von Herman"—*Page 28*

II

PERSONALITY PLUS

THERE are seven stages in the evolution of that individual whose appearance is the signal for a listless " Who-do-you-want-to-see? " from the white-bloused, drab-haired, anæmic little girl who sits in the outer office forever reading last month's magazines. The badge of fear brands the novice. Standing hat in hand, nervous, apprehensive, gulpy, with the elevator door clanging behind him, and the sacred inner door closed before him, he offers up a silent and paradoxical " Thank heaven! " at the office girl's languid " Not in," and dives into the friendly shelter of the next elevator going down. When, at that same message, he can smile, as with a certain grim agreeableness he says, " I'll wait," then has he reached the seventh stage, and taken the orders of the regularly ordained.

Jock McChesney had learned to judge an unknown prospective by glancing at his hall rug and stenographer, which marks the fifth stage. He had learned to regard office boys with something less than white-hot hate. He had learned to let the other fellow do the talking. He had learned to condense a written report into twenty-five words. And he had learned that there was as much difference between the profession of advertising as he had thought of it and advertising as it really was, as there is between a steam calliope and a cathedral pipe organ.

In the big office of the Berg, Shriner Advertising Company they had begun to chuckle a bit over the McChesney solicitor's reports. Those same reports indicated that young McChesney was beginning to find the key to that maddening jumble of complexities known as human nature. Big Sam Hupp, who was the pet caged copy-writing genius of the place, used even to bring an occasional example of Jock's business badinage into the Old Man's office, and the two would grin in secret. As when they ran thus:

Pepsinale Manufacturing Company:
  Mr. Bowser is the kind of gentleman who curses his subordinates in front of the whole office force. Very touchy. Crumpled his advertising manager.

PERSONALITY PLUS

Our chance to get at him is when he is in one of his rare good humors.

Or:

E. V. Kreiss Company:
Kreiss very difficult to reach. Permanent address seems to be Italy, Egypt, and other foreign ports. Occasionally his instructions come from Palm Beach.

At which there rose up before the reader a vision of Kreiss himself — baggy-eyed, cultivated English accent, interested in polo, fast growing contemptuous of things American.

Or still another:

Hodge Manufacturing Company:
Mr. Hodge is a very conservative gentleman. Sits still and lets others do the talking. Has gained quite a reputation for business acumen with this one attribute. Spent $500 last year. Holding his breath preparatory to taking another plunge.

It was about the time that Jock McChesney had got over the novelty of paying for his own clothes, and had begun to talk business in a slightly patronizing way to his clever and secretly amused mother, Mrs. Emma McChesney, secretary of the T. A. Buck Featherloom Petticoat Company, that Sam Hupp noticed a rather cocky over-assurance in Jock's attitude toward the world in general. Whereupon he sent for him.

On Sam Hupp's broad flat desk stood an array of diminutive jars, and bottles, and tiny pots that would have shamed the toilette table of a musical comedy star's dressing-room. There were rose-tinted salves in white bottles. There were white creams in rose-tinted jars. There were tins of ointment and boxes of fragrant soap.

Jock McChesney, entering briskly, eyed the array in some surprise. Then he grinned, and glanced wickedly at Sam Hupp's prematurely bald head.

" No use, Mr. Hupp. They say if it's once gone it's gone. Get a toupee."

" Shut up!" growled Sam Hupp, good-humoredly. " Stay in this game long enough and you'll be a hairless wonder yourself. Ten years ago the girls used to have to tie their hands or wear mittens to keep from running their white fingers through my waving silken locks. Sit down a minute."

Jock reached forward and took up a jar of cream. He frowned in thought. Then:

"Thought I recognized this stuff. Mother uses it. I've seen it on the bathroom shelf."

"You bet she uses it," retorted Sam Hupp. "What's more, millions of other women will be using it in the next few years. This woman," he pointed to the name on the label, "has hit upon the real thing in toilette flub-dub. She's made a little fortune already, and if she don't look out she'll be rich. They've got quite a plant. When she started she used to put the stuff together herself over the kitchen stove. They say it's made of cottage cheese, stirred smooth and tinted pink. Well, anyway they're nationally known now — or will be when they start to advertise right."

"I've seen some of their stuff advertised — somewhere," interrupted Jock, "but I don't remember —"

"There you are. You see the head of this concern is a little bit frightened at the way she seems slated to become a lady cold cream magnate. They say she's scared pink for fear somebody will steal her recipes. She has a kid nephew who acts as general manager, and they're both on the job all the time. They say the lady herself looks like the spinster in a b'gosh drama. You can get a boy to look up your train schedule."

Train! Schedule! Across Jock McChesney's mind there flashed a vision of himself, alert, confident, brisk, taking the luxurious nine o'clock for Philadelphia. Or, maybe, the Limited to Chicago. Dashing down to the station in a taxi, of course. Strolling down the car aisle to take his place among those other thoroughbreds of commerce — men whose chamois gloves and walking sticks, and talk of golf and baseball and motoring spelled elegant leisure, even as their keen eyes and shrewd faces and low-voiced exchange of such terms as " stocks," and " sales " and " propositions " proclaimed them intent on bagging the day's business. Sam Hupp's next words brought him back to reality with a jerk.

" I think you have to change at Buffalo. It gets you to Tonawanda in the morning. Rotten train."

" Tonawanda! " repeated Jock.

" Now listen, kid." Sam Hupp leaned forward, and his eyes behind their great round black-rimmed glasses were intent on Jock. " I'm not going to try to steer you. You think that advertising is a game. It isn't. There are those who think it's a science. But it isn't that either. It's white magic, that's what it is. And you can't learn it from books, any more than you can master trout fishing from reading 'The Complete Angler.'" He swung about and swept the beauty lotions before him in a little heap at the end of his desk. "Here, take this stuff. And get chummy with it. Eat it, if necessary; learn it somehow."

Jock stood up, a little dazed. "But, what! — How? — I mean —"

Sam Hupp glanced up at him. "Sending you down there isn't my idea. It's the Old Man's. He's got an idea that you —" He paused and put a detaining hand on Jock McChesney's arm. "Look here. You think I know a little something about advertising, don't you?"

"You!" laughed Jock. "You're the guy who put the whitening in the Great White Way. Everybody knows you were the —"

"M-m-m, thanks," interrupted Sam Hupp, a little dryly. "Let me tell you something, young 'un. I've got what you might call a thirty-horse-power mind. I keep it running on high all the time, with the muffler cut out, and you can hear me coming for miles. But the Old Man,"— he leaned forward impressively, —" the Old Man, boy, has the eighty-power kind, built like a watch — no smoke, no dripping, and you can't even hear the engine purr. But when he throws her open! Well, he can pass everything on the road. Don't forget that." He turned to his desk again and reached for a stack of papers and cuts. " Good luck to you. If you want any further details you can get 'em from Hayes." He plunged into his work.

There arose in Jock McChesney's mind that instinct of the man in his hour of triumph — the desire to tell a woman of his greatness. He paused a second outside Sam Hupp's office, turned, and walked quickly down the length of the great central room. He stopped before a little glass door at the end, tapped lightly, and entered.

Grace Galt, copy-writer, looked up, frowning a little. Then she smiled. Miss Galt had a complete layout on the desk before her — scrap books, cuts, copy, magazines. There was a little smudge on the end of her nose. Grace

Galt was writing about magnetos. She was writing about magnetos in a way to make you want to drop your customer, or your ironing, or your game, and go downtown and buy that particular kind of magneto at once. Which is the secretest part of the wizardry of advertising copy. To look at Grace Galt you would have thought that she should have been writing about the rose-tinted jars in Jock McChesney's hands instead of about such things as ignition, and insulation, and ball bearings, and induction windings. But it was Grace Galt's gift that she could take just such hard, dry, technical facts and weave them into a story that you followed to the end. She could make you see the romance in condensers and transformers. She had the power that caused the reader to lose himself in the charm of magnetic poles, and ball bearings, and high-tension sparks.

" Just dropped in to say good-by," said Jock, very casually. " Going to run up-state to see the Athena Company — toilette specialties, you know. It ought to be a big account."

" Athena ? " Grace Galt regarded him absently, her mind still on her work. Then her eyes cleared. " You mean at Tonawanda ?

And they're sending you! Well!" She put out a congratulatory hand. Jock gripped it gratefully.

" Not so bad, eh? " he boasted.

" Bad! " echoed Grace Galt. Her face became serious. " Do you realize that there are men in this office who have been here for five years, six years, or even more, and who have never been given a chance to do anything but stenography, or perhaps some private secretarying? "

" I know it," agreed Jock. But there was no humbleness in his tone. He radiated self-satisfaction. He seemed to grow and expand before her eyes. A little shadow of doubt crept across Grace Galt's expression of friendly interest.

" Are you scared," she asked; " just the least bit? "

Jock flushed a little. " Well," he confessed ruefully, " I don't mind telling you I am — a little."

" Good! "

" Good? "

" Yes. The head of that concern is a woman. That's one reason why they didn't send me, I suppose. I — I'd like to say something, if you don't mind."

" Anything you like," said Jock graciously.

" Well, then, don't be afraid of being embarrassed and fussed. If you blush and stammer a little, she'll like it. Play up the coy stuff."

" The coy stuff! " echoed Jock. " I hadn't thought much about my attitude toward the — er — the lady,"— a little stiffly.

" Well, you'd better," answered Miss Galt crisply. She put out her hand in much the same manner as Sam Hupp had used. " Good luck to you. I'll have to ask you to go now. I'm trying to make this magneto sound like something without which no home is complete, and to make people see that there's as much difference between it and every other magneto as there is between the steam shovels that dug out the Panama Canal and the junk that the French left there —" She stopped. Her eyes took on a far-away look. Her lips were parted slightly. " Why, that's not a bad idea — that last. I'll use that. I'll —"

She began to scribble rapidly on the sheet of paper before her. With a jolt Jock Mc-Chesney realized that she had forgotten all about him. He walked quietly to the door, opened it, shut it very quietly, then made for the nearest telephone. He knew one woman he could count on to be proud of him. He gave his number, waited a little eager moment, then:

"Featherloom Petticoat Company? Mrs. McChesney." And waited again. Then he smiled.

"You needn't sound so official," he laughed; "it's only your son. Listen. I "— he took on an elaborate carelessness of tone —" I've got to take a little jump out of town. On business. Oh, a day or so. Rather important though. I'll have time to run up to the flat and throw a few things into a bag. I'll tell you, I really ought to keep a bag packed down here. In case of emergency, you know. What? It's the Athena Toilette Preparations Company. Well, I should say it is! I'll wire you. You bet. Thanks. My what? Oh, toothbrush. No. Good-by."

So it was that at three-ten Jock McChesney took himself, his hopes, his dread, and his smart walrus bag aboard a train that halted and snuffed and backed, and bumped and halted with maddening frequency. But it landed

"With a jolt Jock realized she had forgotten all
about him"—*Page 39*

him at last in a little town bearing the characteristics of all American little towns. It was surprisingly full of six-cylinder cars, and five and ten-cent stores, and banks with Doric columns, and paved streets.

After he had registered at the hotel, and as he was cleaning up a bit, he passed an amused eye over the bare, ugly, fusty little hotel bedroom. But somehow, as he stood in the middle of the room, a graceful, pleasing figure of youth and confidence, the smile faded. Towel in hand he surveyed the barrenness of it. He stared at the impossible wall paper, at the battered furniture, the worn carpet. He sniffed the stuffy smell of — what was that smell, anyhow? — straw, and matting, and dust, and the ghost-odor of hundreds who had occupied the room before him. It came over him with something of a shock that this same sort of room had been his mother's only home in the ten years she had spent on the road as a traveling saleswoman for the T. A. Buck Featherloom Petticoat Company. This was what she had left in the morning. To this she had come back at night. As he stared ahead of him there rose before him a mental picture of her — the brightness of her, the sunni-

[41]

ness, the indomitable energy, and pluck, and
courage. With a sudden burst of new deter-
mination he wadded the towel into a moist ball,
flung it at the washstand, seized hat, coat, and
gloves, and was off down the hall. So it was
with something of his mother's splendid courage
in his heart, but with nothing of her canny
knowledge in his head, Jock McChesney fared
forth to do battle with the merciless god Business.

It was ten-thirty of a brilliant morning just
two days later that a buoyant young figure swung
into an elevator in the great office building that
housed the Berg, Shriner Advertising Company.
Just one more grain of buoyant swing and the
young man's walk might have been termed a
swagger. As it was, his walrus bag just saved
him.

Stepping out of the lift he walked, as
from habit, to the little unlettered door which
admitted employés to the big, bright, inner office. But he did not use it. Instead he turned
suddenly and walked down the hall to the double
door which led into the reception room. He
threw out his legs stiffly and came down rather
flat-footed, the way George Cohan does when

" ' Well, raw-thah ! ' he drawled "—*Page 45*

he's pleased with himself in the second act.

" Hel-lo, Mack! " he called out jovially.

Mack, the usher, so called from his Machiavellian qualities, turned to survey the radiant young figure before him.

" Good morning, Mr. McChesney," he made answer smoothly. Mack never forgot himself. His keen eye saw the little halo of self-satisfaction that hovered above Jock McChesney's head. " A successful trip, I see."

Jock McChesney laughed a little, pleased, conscious laugh. " Well, raw-thah! " he drawled, and opened the door leading into the main office. He had been loath to lose one crumb of the savor of it.

Still smiling, he walked to his own desk, with a nod here and there, dropped his bag, took off coat and hat, selected a cigarette, tapped it smartly, lighted it, and was off down the big room to the little cubby-hole at the other end. But Sam Hupp's plump, keen, good-humored face did not greet him as he entered. The little room was deserted. Frowning, Jock sank into the empty desk chair. He cradled his head in his hands, tilted the chair, pursed his mouth over the slender white cylinder and squinted his eyes up toward the lazy blue spirals of smoke — the very picture of content and satisfaction.

Hupp was in attending some conference in the Old Man's office, of course. He wished they'd hurry. The business of the week was being boiled-down there. Those conferences were great cauldrons into which the day's business, or the week's, was dumped, to be boiled, simmered, stirred, skimmed, cooled. Jock had never been privileged to attend one of these meetings. Perhaps by this time next week he might have a spoon in the stirring too —

There came the murmur of voices as a door was opened. The voices came nearer. Then quick footsteps. Jock recognized them. He rose, smiling. Sam Hupp, vibrating electric energy, breezed in.

" Oh — hello! " he said, surprised. Jock's smile widened to a grin. " You back? "

" Hello, Hupp," he said, coolly. It was the first time that he had omitted the prefix. " You just bet I'm back."

There flashed across Sam Hupp's face a curious little look. The next instant it was gone.

" Well," said Jock, and took a long breath.

" Mr. Berg wants to see you."

Hupp plunged into his work.

"Me? The Old Man wants to see me?"

"Yes," snapped Hupp shortly. Then, in a new tone, "Look here, son. If he says —" He stopped, and turned back to his work again.

"If he says what?"

"Nothing. Better run along."

"What's the hurry? I want to tell you about —"

"Better tell him."

"Oh, all right," said Jock stiffly. If that was the way they treated a fellow who had turned his first real trick, why, very well. He flung out of the little room and made straight for the Old Man's office.

Seated at his great flat table desk, Bartholomew Berg did not look up as Jock entered. This was characteristic of the Old Man. Everything about the chief was deliberate, sure, unhurried. He finished the work in hand as though no other person stood there waiting his pleasure. When at last he raised his massive head he turned his penetrating pale blue eyes full on Jock. Jock was conscious of a little tremor running through him. People were apt to experience that feeling when that steady, unblinking gaze was turned upon them. And yet it was just the clear, unwavering look with which Bartholomew Berg, farmer boy, had been wont to gaze out across the fresh-plowed fields to the horizon beyond which lay the city he dreamed about.

"Tell me your side of it," said Bartholomew Berg tersely.

"All of it?" Jock's confidence was returning.

"Till I stop you."

"Well," began Jock. And standing there at the side of the Old Man's desk, his legs wide apart, his face aglow, his hands on his hips, he plunged into his tale.

"It started off with a bang from the minute I walked into the office of the plant and met Snyder, the advertising manager. We shook hands and sparked — just like that." He snapped thumb and finger. "What do you think! We belong to the same frat! He's '93. Inside of ten minutes he and I were Si-washing around like mad. He introduced me to his aunt. I told her who I was, and all that. But I didn't start off by talking business. We got along from the jump. They both insisted

on showing me through the place. I — well,"
—he laughed a little ruefully,—" there's something about being shown through a factory that
sort of paralyzes my brain. I always feel that
I ought to be asking keen, alert, intelligent ques-
tions like the ones Kipling always asks, or the
Japs when they're taken through the Stock
Yards. But I never can think of any. Well,
we didn't talk business much. But I could see
that they were interested. They seemed to,"
— he faltered and blushed a little,—" to like
me, you know. I played golf with Snyder that
afternoon and he beat me. Won two balls.
The next morning I found there's been a couple
of other advertising men there. And while I
was talking to Snyder — he was telling me
about the time he climbed up and muffled the
chapel bell — that fellow Flynn, of the Dowd
Agency, came in. Snyder excused himself, and
talked to him for — oh, half an hour, perhaps.
But that was all. He was back again in no time.
After that it looked like plain sailing. We got
along wonderfully. When I left I said, ' I expect to know you both better —' "

" I guess," interrupted the Old Man slowly,
" that you'll know them better all right." He

reached out with one broad freckled hand and turned back the page of a desk memorandum. " The Athena account was given to the Dowd Advertising Agency yesterday."

It took Jock McChesney one minute — one long, sickening minute — to grasp the full meaning of it all. He stared at the massive fig- ure before him, his mouth ludicrously open, his eyes round, his breath for the moment sus- pended. Then, in a queer husky voice:

" D'you mean — the Dowd — but — they couldn't —"

" I mean," said Bartholomew Berg, " that you've scored what the dramatic critics call a per- sonal hit; but that doesn't get the box office anything."

" But, Mr. Berg, they said —"

" Sit down a minute, boy." He waved one great heavy hand toward a near-by chair. His eyes were not fixed on Jock. They gazed out of the window toward the great white tower toward which hundreds of thousands of eyes were turned daily — the tower, four-faced but faithful.

" McChesney, do you know why you fell down on that Athena account ? "

"Because I'm an idiot," blurted Jock. "Because I'm a double-barreled, corn-fed, hand-picked chump and —"

"That's one reason," drawled the Old Man grimly. "But it's not the chief one. The real reason why you didn't land that account was because you're too darned charming."

"Charming!" Jock stared.

"Just that. Personality's one of the biggest factors in business to-day. But there are some men who are so likable that it actually counts against them. The client he's trying to convince is so taken with him that he actually forgets the business he represents. We say of a man like that that he is personality plus. Personality is like electricity, McChesney. It's got to be tamed to be useful."

"But I thought," said Jock, miserably, "that the idea was not to talk business all the time."

"You've got it," agreed Berg. "But you must think it all the time. Every minute. It's got to be working away in the back of your head. You know it isn't always the biggest noise that gets the biggest result. The great American hen yields a bigger income than the Steel Trust. Look at Miss Galt. When we have a job that needs a woman's eye do we send her? No. Why? Because she's too blame charming. Too much personality. A man just naturally refuses to talk business to a pretty woman unless she's so smart that —"

" My mother," interrupted Jock, suddenly, and then stopped, surprised at himself.

" Your mother," said Bartholomew Berg slowly, " is one woman in a million. Don't ever forget that. They don't turn out models like Emma McChesney more than once every blue moon."

Jock got to his feet slowly. He felt heavy, old. " I suppose," he began, " that this ends my — my advertising career."

" Ends it!" The Old Man stood up and put a heavy hand on the boy's shoulder. " It only begins it. Unless you want to lie down and quit. Do you? "

" Quit!" cried Jock McChesney. " Quit! Not on your white space!"

" Good!" said Bartholomew Berg, and took Jock McChesney's hand in his own great friendly grasp.

An instinct as strong as that which had made him blatant in his hour of triumph now caused him to avoid, in his hour of defeat, the women-folk before whom he would fain be a hero.   He avoided Grace Galt all that long, dreary after-noon.   He thought wildly of staying down-town for the evening, of putting off the meeting with his mother, of avoiding the dreaded explana-tions, excuses, confessions.

But when he let himself into the flat at five-thirty the place was very quiet, except for Annie, humming in a sort of nasal singsong of content in the kitchen.

He flicked on the light in the living-room.   A new magazine had come.   It lay on the table, its bright cover staring up invitingly.   He ran through its pages.   By force of habit he turned to the back pages.   Ads started back at him — clothing ads, paint ads, motor ads, ads of port-able houses, and vacuum cleaners — and toilette preparations.   He shut the magazine with a vicious slap.

He flicked off the light again, for no reason except that he seemed to like the dusk.   In his own bedroom it was very quiet.

He turned on the light there, too, then turned it off.   He sat down at the edge of his bed. How was it in the stories?   Oh, yes!   The cub always started out on an impossibly difficult business stunt and came back triumphant, to be made a member of the firm at once.

A vision of his own roseate hopes and dreams rose up before him. It grew very dark in the little room, then altogether dark. Then an impudent square of yellow from a light turned on in the apartment next door flung itself on the bedroom floor. Jock stared at it moodily.

A key turned in the lock. A door opened and shut. A quick step. Then: " Jock! " A light flashed in the living-room.

Jock sat up suddenly. He opened his mouth to answer. There issued from his throat a strange and absurd little croak.

" Jock! Home? "

" Yes," answered Jock, and straightened up. But before he could flick on his own light his mother stood in the doorway, a tall, straight, buoyant figure.

" I got your wire and — Why, dear! In the dark! What —"

" Must have fallen asleep, I guess," muttered Jock. Somehow he dreaded to turn on the lights.

And then, very quietly, Emma McChesney

[54]

"... became in some miraculous way a little boy
again "—*Page 57*

came in. She found him, there in the dark, as surely as a mother bear finds her cubs in a cave. She sat down beside him at the edge of the bed and put her hand on his shoulder, and brought his head down gently to her breast. And at that the room, which had been a man's room with its pipe, its tobacco jar, its tie rack filled with cravats of fascinating shapes and hues, became all at once a boy's room again, and the man sitting there with straight, strong shoulders and his little air of worldliness became in some miraculous way a little boy again.

III

DICTATED BUT NOT READ

ABOUT the time that Jock McChesney began to carry a yellow walking-stick down to work each morning his mother noticed a growing tendency on his part to patronize her. Now Mrs. Emma McChesney, successful, capable business woman that she was, could afford to regard her young son's attitude with a quiet and deep amusement. In twelve years Emma McChesney had risen from the humble position of stenographer in the office of the T. A. Buck Featherloom Petticoat Company to the secretaryship of the firm. So when her young son, backed by the profound business knowledge gained in his one year with the Berg, Shriner Advertising Company, hinted gently that her methods and training were archaic, ineffectual, and lacking in those twin condiments known to the twentieth century as pep and ginger, she would listen, eyebrows raised, lower lip caught

[58]

" Jock McChesney began to carry a yellow walking-
stick down to work "— *Page 58*

between her teeth — a trick which gives a distorted expression to the features, calculated to hide any lurking tendency to grin. Besides, though Emma McChesney was forty she looked thirty-two (as business women do), and knew it. Her hard-working life had brought her in contact with people, and things, and events, and had kept her young.

"Thank fortune!" Mrs. McChesney often said, "that I wasn't cursed with a life of ease. These massage-at-ten-fitting-at-eleven-bridge-at-one women always look such hags at thirty-five."

But repetition will ruin the rarest of jokes. As the weeks went on and Jock's attitude persisted, the twinkle in Emma McChesney's eye died. The glow of growing resentment began to burn in its place. Now and then there crept into her eyes a little look of doubt and bewilderment. You sometimes see that same little shocked, dazed expression in the eyes of a woman whose husband has just said, "Isn't that hat too young for you?"

Then, one evening, Emma McChesney's resentment flared into open revolt. She had announced that she intended to rise half an hour earlier each morning in order that she might walk a brisk mile or so on her way down-town, before taking the subway.

" But won't it tire you too much, Mother? " Jock had asked with maddeningly tender solicitude.

His mother's color heightened. Her blue eyes glowed dark.

" Look here, Jock! Will you kindly stop this lean-on-me-grandma stuff! To hear you talk one would think I was ready for a wheel chair and gray woolen bedroom slippers."

" Why, I didn't mean — I only thought that perhaps overexertion in a woman of your — That is, you need your energy for —"

" Don't wallow around in it," snapped Emma McChesney. " You'll only sink in deeper in your efforts to crawl out. I merely want to warn you that if you persist in this pose of tender solicitude for your doddering old mother, I'll — I'll present you with a stepfather a year younger than you. Don't laugh. Perhaps you think I couldn't do it."

" Good Lord, Mother! Of course you don't mean it, but —"

" Mean it! Cleverer women than I have

" ' Good Lord, Mother! Of course you don t mean
it, but —' "— *Page 62*

been driven by their children to marrying bell-boys in self-defense. I warn you!"

That stopped it — for a while. Jock ceased to bestow upon his mother judicious advice from the vast storehouse of his own experience. He refrained from breaking out with elaborate advertising schemes whereby the T. A. Buck Featherloom Petticoat Company might grind every other skirt concern to dust. He gave only a startled look when his mother mischievously suggested raspberry as the color for her new autumn suit. Then, quite suddenly, Circumstance caught Emma McChesney in the meshes and, before she had fought her way free, wrought trouble and change upon her.

Jock McChesney was seated in the window of his mother's office at noon of a brilliant autumn day. A little impatient frown was forming between his eyes. He wanted his luncheon. He had called around expressly to take his mother out to luncheon — always a festive occasion when taken together. But Mrs. McChesney, seated at her desk, was bent absorbedly over a sheet of paper whereon she was adding up two columns of figures at a time — a trick on which

[65]

she rather prided herself. She was counting aloud, her mind leaping agilely, thus:

" Eleven, twenty-nine, forty-three, sixty, sixty-nine —" Her pencil came down on the desk with a thwack. " SIXTY-NINE!" she repeated in capital letters. She turned around to face Jock. " Sixty-nine!" Her voice bristled with indignation. " Now what do you think of that!"

" I think you'd better make it an even seventy, whatever it is you're counting up, and come on out to luncheon. I've an appointment at two-fifteen, you know."

" Luncheon!"— she waved the paper in the air —" with this outrage on my mind! Nectar would curdle in my system."

Jock rose and strolled lazily over to the desk. " What is it?" He glanced idly at the sheet of paper. " Sixty-nine what?"

Mrs. McChesney pressed a buzzer at the side of her desk. " Sixty-nine dollars, that's what! Representing two days' expenses in the six weeks' missionary trip that Fat Ed Meyers just made for us. And in Iowa, too."

" When you gave that fellow the job," began

Jock hotly, " I told you, and Buck told you, that —"

Mrs. McChesney interrupted wearily. " Yes, I know. You'll never have a grander chance to say ' I told you so.' I hired him because he was out of a job and we needed a man who knew the Middle-Western trade, and then because — well, poor fellow, he begged so and promised to keep straight. As though I oughtn't to know that a pinochle-and-poker traveling man can never be anything but a pinochle-and-poker traveling man —"

The office door opened as there appeared in answer to the buzzer a very alert, very smiling, and very tidy office girl. Emma McChesney had tried office boys, and found them wanting.

" Tell Mr. Meyers I want to see him."

" Just going out to lunch,"— she turned like a race horse trembling to be off,—" putting on his overcoat in the front office. Shall I —"

" Catch him."

" Listen here," began Jock uncomfortably; " if you're going to call him perhaps I'd better vanish."

" To save Ed Meyers's tender feelings ! You

don't know him. Fat Ed Meyers could be courtmartialed, tried, convicted, and publicly disgraced, with his epaulets torn off, and his sword broken, and likely as not he'd stoop down, pick up a splinter of steel to use as a toothpick, and Castlewalk down the aisle to the tune with which they were drumming him out of the regiment. Stay right here. Meyers's explanation ought to be at least amusing, if not educating."

In the corridor outside could be heard some one blithely humming in the throaty tenor of the fat man. The humming ceased with a last high note as the door opened and there entered Fat Ed Meyers, rosy, cherubic, smiling, his huge frame looming mountainous in the rippling folds of a loose-hung London plaid topcoat.

"Greetings!" boomed this cheery vision, raising one hand, palm outward, in mystic salute. He beamed upon the frowning Jock. "How's the infant prodigy!" The fact that Jock's frown deepened to a scowl ruffled him not at all. "And what," went on he, crossing his feet and leaning negligently against Mrs. McChesney's desk, "and what can I do for thee, fair lady?"

"For me?" said Emma McChesney, looking up at him through narrowed eyelids. "I'll tell

"Greetings!" — *Page 68*

you what. You can explain to me, in what they
call a few well-chosen words, just how you, or
any other living creature, could manage to turn
in an expense account like that on a six-weeks'
missionary trip through the Middle West."

" Dear lady,"— in the bland tones that one
uses to an unreasonable child,—" you will need
no explanation if you will just remember to lay
the stress on the word missionary. I went forth
through the Middle West to spread the light
among the benighted skirt trade. This wasn't
a selling trip, dear lady. It was a buying ex-
pedition. And I had to buy, didn't I? all the
way from Michigan to Indiana."

He smiled down at her, calm, self-assured, impudent. A little flush grew in Emma McChesney's cheeks.

" I've always said," she began, crisply, " that
one could pretty well judge a man's character,
temperament, morals, and physical make-up by
just glancing at his expense account. The
trouble with you is that you haven't learned the
art of spending money wisely. It isn't always
the man with the largest expense sheet that gets
the most business. And it isn't the man who
leaves the greatest number of circles on the table

top in his hotel room, either." She paused a moment. Ed Meyers's smile had lost some of its heartiness. " Mr. Buck's out of town, as you know. He'll be back next week. He wasn't in favor of —"

" Now, Mrs. McChesney," interrupted Ed Meyers nervously, " you know there's always one live one in every firm, just like there's always one star in every family. You're the —"

" I'm the one who wants to know how you could spend sixty-nine dollars for two days' incidentals in Iowa. Iowa! Why, look here, Ed Meyers, I made Iowa for ten years when I was on the road. You know that. And you know, and I know, that in order to spend sixty-nine dollars for incidentals in two days in Iowa you have to call out the militia."

" Not when you're trying to win the love of every skirt buyer from Sioux City to Des Moines."

Emma McChesney rose impatiently. " Oh, that's nonsense! You don't need to do that these days. Those are old-fashioned methods. They're out of date. They —"

At that a little sound came from Jock.

Emma heard it, glanced at him, turned away again in confusion.

"I was foolish enough in the first place to give you this job for old times' sake," she continued hurriedly.

Fat Ed Meyers' face drooped dolefully. He cocked his round head on one side fatuously. "For old times' sake," he repeated, with tremulous pathos, and heaved a gusty sigh.

"Which goes to show that I need a guardian," finished Emma McChesney cruelly. "The only old times that I can remember are when I was selling Featherlooms, and you were out for the Sans-Silk Skirt Company, both covering the same territory, and both running a year-around race to see which could beat the other at his own game. The only difference was that I always played fair, while you played low-down whenever you had a chance."

"Now, my dear Mrs. McChesney —"

"That'll be all," said Emma McChesney, as one whose patience is fast slipping away. "Mr. Buck will see you next week." Then, turning to her son as the door closed on the drooping figure of the erstwhile buoyant Meyers, "Where'll we lunch, Jock?"

"Mother," Jock broke out hotly, "why in the name of all that's foolish do you persist in using the methods of Methuselah! People don't sell goods any more by sending out fat old ex-traveling men to jolly up the trade."

"Jock," repeated Emma McChesney slowly, "where — shall — we — lunch?"

It was a grim little meal, eaten almost in silence. Emma McChesney had made it a rule to use luncheon time as a recess. She played mental tag and hop-scotch, so that, returning to her office refreshed in mind and body, she could attack the afternoon's work with new vigor. And never did she talk or think business.

To-day she ate her luncheon with a forced appetite, glanced about with a listlessness far removed from her usual alert interest, and followed Jock's attempts at conversation with a polite effort that was more insulting than downright inattention.

"Dessert, Mother?" Jock had to say it twice before she heard.

"What? Oh, no — I think not."

The waiter hesitated, coughed discreetly, lifted his eyebrows insinuatingly. "The French pastry's particularly nice to-day, madam.

If you'd care to try something? Eclair, madam
— peach tart — mocha tart — caramel —"

Emma McChesney smiled. " It does sound
tempting." She glanced at Jock. " And we're
wearing our gowns so floppy this year that it
makes no difference whether one's fat or not."
She turned to the waiter. " I never can tell
till I see them. Bring your pastry tray, will
you? "

Jock McChesney's finger and thumb came together with a snap. He leaned across the table
toward his mother, eyes glowing, lips parted
and eager. " There! you've proved my point."

" Point? "

" About advertising. No, don't stop me.
Don't you see that what applies to pastry applies to petticoats? You didn't think of French
pastry until he suggested it to you — advertised
it, really. And then you wanted a picture of
them. You wanted to know what they looked
like before buying. That's all there is to advertising. Telling people about a thing, making 'em want it, and showing 'em how it will
look when they have it. Get me? "

Emma McChesney was gazing at Jock with
a curious, fascinated stare. It was a blank lit-

tle look, such as we sometimes wear when the mind is working furiously. If the insinuating waiter, presenting the laden tray for her inspection, was startled by the rapt expression which she turned upon the cunningly wrought wares, he was too much a waiter to show it.

A pause. " That one," said Mrs. McChesney, pointing to the least ornate. She ate it, down to the last crumb, in a silence that was pregnant with portent. She put down her fork and sat back.

" Jock, you win. I — I suppose I have fallen out of step. Perhaps I've been too busy watching my own feet. T. A. will be back next week. Could your office have an advertising plan roughly sketched by that time ? "

" Could they ! " His tone was exultant. " Watch 'em ! Hupp's been crazy to make Featherlooms famous."

" But look here, son. I want a hand in that copy. I know Featherlooms better than your Sam Hupp will ever —"

Jock shook his head. " They won't stand for that, Mother. It never works. The manufacturer always thinks he can write magic stuff because he knows his own product. But he never can. You see, he knows too much. That's it. No perspective."

" We'll see," said Emma McChesney curtly.

So it was that ten days later the first important conference in the interests of the Featherloom Petticoat Company's advertising campaign was called. But in those ten days of hurried preparation a little silent tragedy had come about. For the first time in her brave, sunny life Emma McChesney had lost faith in herself. And with such malicious humor does Fate work her will that she chose Sam Hupp's new dictagraph as the instrument with which to prick the bubble of Mrs. McChesney's self-confidence.

Sam Hupp, one of the copy-writing marvels of the Berg, Shriner firm, had a trick of forgetting to shut off certain necessary currents when he paused in his dictation to throw in conversational asides. The old and experienced stenographers, had learned to look out for that, and to eliminate from their typewritten letters certain irrelevant and sometimes irreverent asides which Sam Hupp evidently had addressed to his pipe, or the office boy, and not intended for the tube of the all-devouring dictagraph.

There was a new and nervous little stenographer in the outer office, and she had not been warned of this.

"We think very highly of the plan you suggest," Sam Hupp had said into the dictagraph's mouthpiece. "In fact, in one of your valuable copy suggestions you —"

Without changing his tone he glanced over his shoulder at his colleague, Hopper, who was listening and approving.

" . . . Let the old girl think the idea is her own. She's virtually the head of that concern, and they've spoiled her. Successful, and used to being kowtowed to. Doesn't know her notions of copy are ten years behind the advertising game —"

And went on with his letter again. After which he left the office to play golf. And the little blond numbskull in the outer office dutifully took down what the instrument had to say, word for word, marked it, "Dictated, but not read," signed neat initials, and with a sigh went on with the rest of her sheaf of letters.

Emma McChesney read the letter next morning. She read it down to the end, and then again. The two readings were punctuated with a little gasp, such as we give when an icy douche

[78]

is suddenly turned upon us. And that was all.

A week later an intent little group formed a ragged circle about the big table in the private office of Bartholomew Berg, head of the Berg, Shriner Advertising Company. Bartholomew Berg himself, massive, watchful, taciturn, managing to give an impression of power by his very silence, sat at one side of the long table. Just across from him a sleek-haired stenographer bent over her note book, jotting down every word, that the conference might make business history. Hopper, at one end of the room, studied his shoe heel intently. He was unbelievably boyish looking to command the fabulous salary reported to be his. Advertising men, mentioning his name, pulled a figurative forelock as they did so. Near Mrs. McChesney sat Sam Hupp, he of the lightning brain and the sure-fire copy. Emma McChesney, strangely silent, kept her eyes intent on the faces of the others. T. A. Buck, interested, enthusiastic, but somewhat uncertain, glanced now and then at his silent business partner, found no satisfaction in her set face, and glanced away again. Grace Galt, unbelievably young and pretty to have won a place for herself in that conference of business people, smiled in secret at Jock McChesney's evident struggle to conceal his elation at being present at this, his first staff meeting.

The conference had lasted one hour now. In that time Featherloom petticoats had been picked to pieces, bit by bit, from hem to waistband. Nothing had been left untouched. Every angle had come under the keen vision of the advertising experts — the comfort of the garment, its durability, style, cheapness, service. Which to emphasize?

" H—m, novelty campaign, in my opinion," said Hopper, breaking one of his long silences. " There's nothing new in petticoats themselves, you know. You've got to give 'em a new angle."

" Yep," agreed Hupp. " Start out with a feature skirt. Might illustrate with one of those freak drawings they're crazy about now — slinky figure, you know, hollow-chested, one foot trailing, and all that. They're crazy, but they do attract attention, no doubt of that."

Bartholomew Berg turned his head slowly. " What's your opinion, Mrs. McChesney? " he asked.

DICTATED BUT NOT READ

" I — I'm afraid I haven't any," said Emma McChesney listlessly. T. A. Buck stared at her in dismay and amazement.

" How about you, Mr. Buck? "

" Why — I — er — of course this advertising game's new to me. I'm really leaving it in your hands. I really thought that Mrs. McChesney's idea was to make a point of the fact that these petticoats were not freak petticoats, but skirts for the everyday women. She gave me what I thought was a splendid argument a week ago." He turned to her helplessly.

Mrs. McChesney sat silent.

Bartholomew Berg leaned forward a little and smiled one of his rare smiles.

" Won't you tell us, Mrs. McChesney? We'd all like to hear what you have to say."

Mrs. McChesney looked down at her hands. Then she looked up, and addressed what she had to say straight to Bartholomew Berg.

" I — simply didn't want to interfere in this business. I know nothing about it, really. Of course, I do know Featherloom petticoats. I know all about them. It seemed to me that just because the newspapers and magazines were full of pictures showing spectacular creatures in impossible attitudes wearing tango tea skirts, we are apt to forget that those types form only a thin upper crust, and that down beneath there are millions and millions of regular, everyday women doing regular everyday things in regular everyday clothes. Women who wash on Monday, and iron on Tuesday, and bake one-egg cakes, and who have to hurry home to get supper when they go down-town in the afternoon. They're the kind who go to market every morning, and take the baby along in the go-cart, and they're not wearing crêpe de chine tango petticoats to do it in, either. They're wearing skirts with a drawstring in the back, and a label in the band, guaranteed to last one year. Those are the people I'd like to reach, and hold."

" Hm! " said Hopper, from his corner, cryptically.

Bartholomew Berg looked at Emma McChesney admiringly. " Sounds reasonable and logical," he said.

Sam Hupp sat up with a jerk.

" It does sound reasonable," he said briskly. " But it isn't. Pardon me, won't you, Mrs. McChesney? But you must realize that this is an extravagant age. The very workingmen's wives have caught the spending fever. The time is past when you can attract people to your goods with the promise of durability and wear. They don't expect goods to wear. They'd resent it if they did. They get tired of an article before it's worn out. They're looking for novelties. They'd rather get two months' wear out of a skirt that's slashed a new way, than a year's wear out of one that looks like the sort that mother used to make."

Mrs. McChesney, her cheeks very pink, her eyes very bright, subsided into silence. In silence she sat throughout the rest of the conference. In silence she descended in the elevator with T. A. Buck, and in silence she stepped into his waiting car.

T. A. Buck eyed her worriedly. "Well?" he said. Then, as Mrs. McChesney shrugged noncommittal shoulders, "Tell me, how do you feel about it?"

Emma McChesney turned to face him, breathing rather quickly.

"The last time I felt as I do just now was when Jock was a baby. He took sick, and the doctors were puzzled. They thought it might be something wrong with his spine. They had

PERSONALITY PLUS

a consultation — five of them — with the poor little chap on the bed, naked. They wouldn't let me in, so I listened in the hallway, pressed against the door with my face to the crack. They prodded him, and poked him, and worked his little legs and arms, and every time he cried I prayed, and wept, and clawed the door with my fingers, and called them beasts and torturers and begged them to let me in, though I wasn't conscious that I was doing those things — at the time. I didn't know what they were doing to him, though they said it was all for his good, and they were only trying to help him. But I only knew that I wanted to rush in, and grab him up in my arms, and run away with him — run, and run, and run."

She stopped, lips trembling, eyes suspiciously bright.

"And that's the way I felt in there — this afternoon."

T. A. Buck reached up and patted her shoulder. "Don't, old girl! It's going to work out splendidly, I'm sure. After all, those chaps do know best."

"They may know best, but they don't know Featherlooms," retorted Emma McChesney.

"True. But perhaps what Jock said when he walked with us to the elevator was pretty nearly right. You know he said we were criticising their copy the way a plumber would criticise the Parthenon — so busy finding fault with the lack of drains that we failed to see the beauty of the architecture."

"T. A.," said Emma McChesney solemnly, "T. A., we're getting old."

"Old! You! I! Ha!"

"You may 'Ha!' all you like. But do you know what they thought of us in there? They thought we were a couple of fogies, and they humored us, that's what they did. I'll tell you, T. A., when the time comes for me to give Jock up to some little pink-faced girl I'll do it, and smile if it kills me. But to hand my Featherlooms over to a lot of cold-blooded experts who — well —" she paused, biting her lip.

"We'll see, Emma; we'll see."

They did see. The Featherloom petticoat campaign was launched with a great splash. It sailed serenely into the sea of national business. Then suddenly something seemed to go wrong with its engines. It began to wobble and showed a decided list to port. Jock, who at the beginning was so puffed with pride that his gold fountain pen threatened to burst the confines of his very modishly tight vest, lost two degrees of pompousness a day, and his attitude toward his unreproachful mother was almost humble.

A dozen times a week T. A. Buck would stroll casually into Mrs. McChesney's office. "Think it's going to take hold?" he would ask. "Our men say the dealers have laid in, but the public doesn't seem to be tearing itself limb from limb to get to our stuff."

Emma McChesney would smile, and shrug noncommittal shoulders.

When it became very painfully apparent that it wasn't "taking hold," T. A. Buck, after asking the same question, now worn and frayed with asking, broke out, crossly:

"Well, really, I don't mind the shrug, but I do wish you wouldn't smile. After all, you know, this campaign is costing us money — real money, and large chunks of it. It's very evident that we shouldn't have tried to make a national campaign of this thing."

Whereupon Mrs. McChesney's smile grew into a laugh. "Forgive me, T. A. I'm not laughing at you. I'm laughing because — well, I can't tell you why. It's a woman's reason, and you wouldn't think it a reason at all. For that matter, I suppose it isn't, but — Anyway, I've got something to tell you. The fault of this campaign has been the copy. It was perfectly good advertising, but it left the public cold. When they read those ads they might have been impressed with the charm of the garment, but it didn't fill their breasts with any wild longing to possess one. It didn't make the women feel unhappy until they had one of those skirts hanging on the third hook in their closet. The only kind of advertising that is advertising is the kind that makes the reader say, ' I'll have one of those.' "

T. A. Buck threw out helpless hands. " What are we going to do about it ? "

" Do? I've already done it."

" Done what ? "

" Written the kind of copy that I think Featherlooms ought to have. I just took my knowledge of Featherlooms, plus what I knew about human nature, sprinkled in a handful of good humor and sincerity, and they're going to feed it to the public. It's the same recipe that

PERSONALITY PLUS

I used to use in selling Featherlooms on the road. It used to go by word of mouth. I don't see why it shouldn't go on paper. It isn't classic advertising. It isn't scientific. It isn't even what they call psychological, I suppose. But it's human. And it's going to reach that great, big, solid, safe, spot-cash mass known as the middle class. Of course my copy may be wrong. It may not go, after all, but —"

But it did go. It didn't go with a rush, or a bang. It went slowly, surely, hand over hand, but it went, and it kept on going. And watching it climb and take hold there came back to Emma McChesney's eye the old sparkle, to her step the old buoyancy, to her voice the old delightful ring. And now, when T. A. Buck strolled into her office of a morning, with his, "It's taking hold, Mrs. Mack," she would dimple like a girl as she laughed back at him —

"With a grip that won't let go."

"It looks very much as though we were going to be millionaires in our old age, you and I?" went on Buck.

Emma McChesney opened her eyes wide.

"Old!" she mocked, "Old! You! I! Ha!"

IV

THE MAN WITHIN HIM

THEY used to do it much more pictur-
esquely. They rode in coats of scarlet,
in the crisp, clear morning, to the winding of
horns and the baying of hounds, to the thud-
thud of hoofs, and the crackle of underbrush.
Across fresh-plowed fields they went, crashing
through forest paths, leaping ditches, taking
fences, scrambling up the inclines, pelting down
the hillside, helter-skelter, until, panting, wide-
eyed, eager, blood-hungry, the hunt closed in at
the death.

The scarlet coat has sobered down to the
somber gray and the snuffy brown of that un-
romantic garment known as the business suit.
The winding horn is become a goblet, and its
notes are the tinkle of ice against glass. The
baying of hounds has harshened to the squawk
of the motor siren. The fresh-plowed field is
a blue print, the forest maze a roll of plans and

specifications. Each fence is a business barrier.
Every ditch is of a competitor's making, dug
craftily so that the clumsy-footed may come a
cropper. All the romance is out of it, all the
color, all the joy. But two things remain the
same: The look in the face of the hunter as
he closed in on the fox is the look in the face of
him who sees the coveted contract lying ready
for the finishing stroke of his pen. And his
words are those of the hunter of long ago as,
eyes a-gleam, teeth bared, muscles still taut with
the tenseness of the chase, he waves the paper
high in air and cries, " I've made a killing! "

For two years Jock McChesney had watched
the field as it swept by in its patient, devious,
cruel game of Hunt the Contract. But he had
never been in at the death. Those two years
had taught him how to ride; to take a fence;
to leap a ditch. He had had his awkward
bumps, and his clumsy falls. He had lost his
way more than once. But he had always
groped his way back again, stumblingly, through
the dusk. Jock McChesney was the youngest
man on the Berg, Shriner Advertising Company's big staff of surprisingly young men. So
young that the casual glance did not reveal to

you the marks that the strain of those two years had left on his boyish face. But the marks were there.

Nature etches with the most delicate of points. She knows the cunning secret of light and shadow. You scarcely realize that she has been at work. A faint line about the mouth, a fairy tracing at the corners of the eyes, a mere vague touch just at the nostrils — and the thing is done.

Even Emma McChesney's eyes — those mother-eyes which make the lynx seem a mole — had failed to note the subtle change. Then, suddenly, one night, the lines leaped out at her.

They were seated at opposite sides of the book-littered library table in the living-room of the cheerful up-town apartment which was the realization of the nightly dream which Mrs. Emma McChesney had had in her ten years on the road for the T. A. Buck Featherloom Petticoat Company. Jock McChesney's side of the big table was completely covered with the mass of copy-paper, rough sketches, photographs and drawings which make up an advertising lay-out. He was bent over the work, absorbed, intent, his forearms resting on the table. Emma McChesney glanced up from her magazine just as Jock bent forward to reach a scrap of paper that had fluttered away. The lamplight fell full on his face. And Emma McChesney saw. The hand that held the magazine fell to her lap. Her lips were parted slightly. She sat very quietly, her eyes never leaving the face that frowned so intently over the littered table. The room had been very quiet before — Jock busy with his work, his mother interested in her magazine. But this silence was different. There was something electric in it. It was a silence that beats on the brain like a noise. Jock McChesney, bent over his work, heard it, felt it, and, oppressed by it, looked up suddenly. He met those two eyes opposite.

" Spooks? Or is it my godlike beauty which holds you thus? Or is my face dirty? "

Emma McChesney did not smile. She laid her magazine on the table, face down, and leaned forward, her staring eyes still fixed on her son's face.

" Look here, young 'un. Are you working too hard? "

" Me? Now? This stuff you mean — ? "

[92]

" No; I mean in the last year. Are they piling it up on you?"

Jock laughed a laugh that was nothing less than a failure, so little of real mirth did it contain.

" Piling it up! Lord, no! I wish they would. That's the trouble. They don't give me a chance."

" A chance! Why, that's not true, son. You've said yourself that there are men who have been in the office three times as long as you have, who never have had the opportunities that they've given you."

It was as though she had touched a current that thrilled him to action. He pushed back his chair and stood up, one hand thrust into his pocket, the other passing quickly over his head from brow to nape with a quick, nervous gesture that was new to him.

" And why!" he flung out. " Why! Not because they like the way I part my hair. They don't do business that way up there. It's because I've made good, and those other dubs haven't. That's why. They've let me sit in at the game. But they won't let me take any tricks. I've been an apprentice hand for two

years now. I'm tired of it. I want to be in on
a killing. I want to taste blood. I want a
chance at some of the money — real money."

Emma McChesney sat back in her chair and
surveyed the angry figure before her with quiet,
steady eyes.

"I might have known that only one thing
could bring those lines into your face, son."
She paused a moment. "So you want money
as badly as all that, do you?"

Jock's hand came down with a thwack on the
papers before him.

"Want it! You just bet I want it."

"Do I know her?" asked Emma McChesney quietly.

Jock stopped short in his excited pacing up
and down the room.

"Do you know — Why, I didn't say
there — What makes you think that —?"

"When a youngster like you, whose greatest
worry has been whether Harvard'll hold 'em
again this year, with Baxter out, begins to howl
about not being appreciated in business, and to
wear a late fall line of wrinkles where he has
been smooth before, I feel justified in saying,
'Do I know her?'"

" Well, it isn't any one — at least, it isn't what you mean you think it is when you say you —"

" Careful there! You'll trip. Never you mind what I mean I think it is when I say. Count ten, and then just tell me what you think you mean."

Jock passed his hand over his head again with that nervous little gesture. Then he sat down, a little wearily. He stared moodily down at the pile of papers before him. His mother faced him quietly across the table.

" Grace Galt's getting twice as much as I am," Jock broke out, with savage suddenness. " The first year I didn't mind. A fellow gets accustomed, these days, to see women breaking into all the professions and getting away with men-size salaries. But her pay check doubles mine — more than doubles it."

" It's been my experience," observed Emma McChesney, " that when a firm condescends to pay a woman twice as much as a man, that means she's worth six times as much."

A painful red crept into Jock's face. " Maybe. Two years ago that would have sounded reasonable to me. Two years ago, when I walked down Broadway at night, a fifty-foot electric sign at Forty-second was just an electric sign to me. Just part of the town's decoration like the chorus girls, and the midnight theater crowds. Now — well, now every blink of every red and yellow globe is crammed full of meaning. I know the power that advertising has; how it influences our manners, and our morals, and our minds, and our health. It regulates the food we eat, and the clothes we wear, and the books we read, and the entertainment we seek. It's colossal, that's what it is! It's —"

" Keep on like that for another two years, sonny, and no business banquet will be complete without you. The next thing you know you'll be addressing the Y. M. C. A. advertising classes on The Young Man in Business."

Jock laughed a rueful little laugh. " I didn't mean to make a speech. I was just trying to say that I've served my apprenticeship. It hurts a fellow's pride. You can't hold your head up before a girl when you know her salary's twice yours, and you know that she knows it. Why look at Mrs. Hoffman, who's with the Dowd Agency. Of course she's a wonder, even if her

face does look like the fifty-eighth variety.
She can write copy that lifts a campaign
right out of the humdrum class, and makes it
luminous.   Her husband works in a bank somewhere.   He earns about as much as Mrs. Hoffman pays the least of her department subordinates.   And he's so subdued that he side-steps
when he walks, and they call him the human
jelly-fish."

Emma McChesney was regarding her son
with a little puzzled frown.   Suddenly she
reached out and tapped the topmost of the scrib-
bled sheets strewn the length of Jock's side of
the table.

" What's all this ? "

Jock tipped back his chair and surveyed the
clutter before him.

" That," said he, " is what is known on the
stage as ' the papers.'   And it's the real plot of
this piece."

" M-m-m — I thought so.   Just favor me
with a scenario, will you ? "

Half-grinning, half-serious, Jock stuck his
thumbs in the armholes of his waistcoat, and
began.

" Scene: Offices of the Berg, Shriner Advertising Company. Time, the present. Characters: Jock McChesney, handsome, daring, brilliant —"

"Suppose you — er — skip the characters, however fascinating, and get to the action."

Jock McChesney brought the tipped chair down on all-fours with a thud, and stood up. The grin was gone. He was as serious as he had been in the midst of his tirade of five minutes before.

"All right. Here it is. And don't blame me if it sounds like cheap melodrama. This stuff," and he waved a hand toward the paper-laden table, "is an advertising campaign plan for the Griebler Gum Company, of St. Louis. Oh, don't look impressed. The office hasn't handed me any such commission. I just got the idea like a flash, and I've been working it out for the last two weeks. It worked itself out, almost — the way a really scorching idea does, sometimes. This Griebler has been advertising for years. You know the Griebler gum. But it hasn't been the right sort of advertising. Old Griebler, the original gum man, had fogy notions about advertising, and as long as he lived they had to keep it down. He died a few months ago — you must have read of it. Left a regular mint. Ben Griebler, the oldest son, started right in to clean out the cobwebs. Of course the advertising end of it has come in for its share of the soap and water. He wants to make a clean sweep of it. Every advertising firm in the country has been angling for the contract. It's going to be a real one. Two-thirds of the crowd have submitted plans. And that's just where my kick comes in. The Berg, Shriner Company makes it a rule never to submit advance plans."

" Excuse me if I seem a trifle rude," interrupted Mrs. McChesney, " but I'd like to know where you think you've been wronged in this."

" Right here! " replied Jock, and he slapped his pocket, " and here," he pointed to his head. " Two spots so vital that they make old Achilles's heel seem armor-plated. Ben Griebler is one of the show-me kind. He wants value received for money expended, and while everybody knows that he has a loving eye on the Berg, Shriner crowd, he won't sign a thing until he knows what he's getting. A firm's record, standing, staff, equipment, mean nothing to him."

" But, Jock, I still don't see —"

Jock gathered up a sheaf of loose papers and brandished them in the air. " This is where I come in. I've got a plan here that will fetch this Griebler person. Oh, I'm not dreaming. I outlined it for Sam Hupp, and he was crazy about it. Sam Hupp had some sort of plan outlined himself. But he said this made his sound as dry as cigars in Denver. And you know yourself that Sam Hupp's copy is so brilliant that he could sell brewery advertising to a temperance magazine."

Emma McChesney stood up. She looked a little impatient, and a trifle puzzled. " But why all this talk! I don't get you. Take your plan to Mr. Berg. If it's what you think it is he'll see it quicker than any other human being, and he'll probably fall on your neck and invest you in royal robes and give you a mahogany desk all your own."

" Oh, what's the good! " retorted Jock disgustedly. " This Griebler has an appointment at the office to-morrow. He'll be closeted with the Old Man. They'll call in Hupp. But never a plan will they reveal. It's against their code of ethics. Ethics! I'm sick of the word.

JAMES MONTGOMERY FLAGG

" She laid one hand very lightly on his arm and looked
up into the sullen, angry young face "— *Page 103*

THE MAN WITHIN HIM

I suppose you'd say I'm lucky to be associated
with a firm like that, and I suppose I am. But
I wish in the name of all the gods of Business
that they weren't so bloomin' conservative.
Ethics! They're all balled up in 'em, like
Henry James in his style."

Emma McChesney came over from her side
of the table and stood very close to her son.
She laid one hand very lightly on his arm
and looked up into the sullen, angry young
face.

" I've seen older men than you are, Jock, and
better men, and bigger men, wearing that same
look, and for the same reason. Every ambi-
tious man or woman in business wears it at one
time or another. Sooner or later, Jock, you'll
have your chance at the money end of this
game. If you don't care about the thing you
call ethics, it'll be sooner. If you do care, it
will be later. It rests with you, but it's bound
to come, because you've got the stuff in you."

" Maybe," replied Jock the cynical. But
his face lost some of its sullenness as he looked
down at that earnest, vivid countenance up-
turned to his. " Maybe. It sounds all right,
Mother — in the story books. But I'm not

quite solid on it. These days it isn't so much
what you've got in you that counts as what you
can bring out. I know the young man's slogan
used to be 'Work and Wait,' or something
pretty like that. But these days they've boiled
it down to one word — ' Produce '! "

" The marvel of it is that there aren't more
of 'em," observed Emma McChesney sadly.

" More what? "

" More lines. Here,"— she touched his
forehead,—" and here,"— she touched his
eyes.

" Lines! " Jock swung to face a mirror.
" Good! I'm so infernally young-looking that
no one takes me seriously. It's darned hard
trying to convince people you're a captain of
finance when you look like an errand boy."

From the center of the room Mrs. McChesney watched the boy as he surveyed himself in
the glass. And as she gazed there came a
frightened look into her eyes. It was gone in
a minute, and in its place came a curious little
gleam, half amused, half pugnacious.

" Jock McChesney, if I thought that you
meant half of what you've said to-night about
honor, and ethics, and all that, I'd —"

[104]

" Spank me, I suppose," said the young six-footer.

" No," and all the humor had fled, " I — Jock, I've never said much to you about your father. But I think you know that he was what he was to the day of his death. You were just about eight when I made up my mind that life with him was impossible. I said then — and you were all I had, son — that I'd rather see you dead than to have you turn out to be a son of your father. Don't make me remember that wish, Jock."

Two quick steps and his arms were about her. His face was all contrition. " Why — Mother! I didn't mean — You see this is business, and I'm crazy to make good, and it's such a fight —"

" Don't I know it? " demanded Emma Mc-Chesney. " I guess your mother hasn't been sitting home embroidering lunchcloths these last fifteen years." She lifted her head from the boy's shoulder. " And now, son, considering me, not as your doting mother, but in my business capacity as secretary of the T. A. Buck Featherloom Petticoat Company, suppose you reveal to me the inner workings of this plan of yours. I'd like to know if you really are the advertising wizard that you think you are."

So it was that long after Annie's dinner dishes had ceased to clatter in the kitchen; long after she had put her head in at the door to ask, " Aigs 'r cakes for breakfast? " long after those two busy brains should have rested in sleep, the two sat at either side of the light-flooded table, the face of one glowing as he talked, the face of the other sparkling as she listened. And at midnight:

" Why, you infant wonder! " exclaimed Emma McChesney.

At nine o'clock next morning when Jock McChesney entered the offices of the Berg, Shriner Advertising Company he carried a flat, compact bundle of papers under his arm encased in protecting covers of pasteboard, and further secured by bands of elastic. This he carried to his desk, deposited in a drawer, and locked the drawer.

By eleven o'clock the things which he had predicted the night before had come to pass. A plump little man, with a fussy manner and Western clothes had been ushered into Bartholomew Berg's private office. Instinct told him that this was Griebler. Jock left his desk and strolled up to get the switchboard operator's confirmation of his guess. Half an hour later Sam Hupp hustled by and disappeared into the Old Man's sanctum.

Jock fingered the upper left-hand drawer of his desk. The maddening blankness of that closed door! If only he could find some excuse for walking into that room — any old excuse, no matter how wild! — just to get a chance at it —

His telephone rang. He picked up the receiver, his eye on the closed door, his thoughts inside that room.

" Mr. Berg wants to see you right away," came the voice of the switchboard operator.

Something seemed to give way inside — something in the region of his brain — no, his heart — no, his lungs —

" Well, can you beat that! " said Jock McChesney aloud, in a kind of trance of joy. " Can — you — beat — that! "

Then he buttoned the lower button of his coat, shrugged his shoulders with an extra wriggle at the collar (the modern hero's method of girding up his loins), and walked

calmly into Bartholomew Berg's very private
office.

In the second that elapsed between the opening and the closing of the door Jock's glance
swept the three men — Bartholomew Berg,
quiet, inscrutable, seated at his great table-
desk; Griebler, lost in the depths of a great
leather chair, smoking fussily and twitching with
a hundred little restless, irritating gestures;
Sam Hupp, standing at the opposite side of the
room, hands in pockets, attitude argumentative.

" This is Mr. McChesney," said Bartholomew Berg. " Mr. Griebler, McChesney."

Jock came forward, smiling that charming
smile of his. " Mr. Griebler," he said, extend-
ing his hand, " this is a great pleasure."

" Hm! " growled Ben Griebler, " I didn't
know they picked 'em so young."

His voice was a piping falsetto that somehow
seemed to match his restless little eyes.

Jock thrust his hands hurriedly into his
pockets. He felt his face getting scarlet.

" They're — ah — using 'em young this
year," said Bartholomew Berg. His voice
sounded bigger, and smoother, and pleasanter
than ever in contrast with that other's shrill

tone. " I prefer 'em young, myself. You'll never catch McChesney using ' in the last analysis ' to drive home an argument. He has a new idea about every nineteen minutes, and every other one's a good one, and every nineteenth or so's an inspiration." The Old Man laughed one of his low, chuckling laughs.

" Hm — that so ? " piped Ben Griebler. " Up in my neck of the woods we aren't so long on inspiration. We're just working men, and we wear working clothes —"

" Oh, now," protested Berg, his eyes twinkling, " McChesney's necktie and socks and handkerchief may form one lovely, blissful color scheme, but that doesn't signify that his advertising schemes are not just as carefully and arttistically blended."

Ben Griebler looked shrewdly up at Jock through narrowed lids. " Maybe. I'll talk to you in a minute, young man — that is —" he turned quickly upon Berg —" if that isn't against your crazy principles, too ? "

" Why, not at all," Bartholomew Berg assured him. " Not at all. You do me an injustice."

Griebler moved up closer to the broad table.

The two fell into a low-voiced talk.
Jock looked rather helplessly around at Sam
Hupp. That alert gentleman was signaling
him frantically with head and wagging finger.
Jock crossed the big room to Hupp's side. The
two moved off to a window at the far end.

"Give heed to your Unkie," said Sam Hupp,
talking very rapidly, very softly, and out of one
corner of his mouth. "This Griebler's looking for an advertising manager. He's as pig-
headed as a — a — well, as a pig, I suppose.
But it's a corking chance, youngster, and the
Old Man's just recommended you — strong.
Now —"

"Me —!" exploded Jock.

"Shut up!" hissed Hupp. "Two or three
years with that firm would be the making of you
— if you made good, of course. And you
could. They want to move their factory here
from St. Louis within the next few years. Now
listen. When he talks to you, you play up the
keen, alert stuff with a dash of sophistication,
see? If you can keep your mouth shut and
throw a kind of a canny, I-get-you, look into
your eyes, all the better. He's gabby enough
for two. Try a line of talk that is filled with

[110]

the fire and enthusiasm of youth, combined with the good judgment and experience of middle age, and you've —"

" Say, look here," stammered Jock. " Even if I was Warfield enough to do all that, d'you honestly think — me an advertising manager! — with a salary that Griebler —"

" You nervy little shrimp, go in and win. He'll pay five thousand if he pays a cent. But he wants value for money expended. Now I've tipped you off. You make your killing —"

" Oh, McChesney! " called Bartholomew Berg, glancing round.

" Yes, sir! " said Jock, and stood before him in the same moment.

" Mr. Griebler is looking for a competent, enthusiastic, hard-working man as advertising manager. I've spoken to him of you. I know what you can do. Mr. Griebler might trust my judgment in this, but —"

" I'll trust my own judgment," snapped Ben Griebler. " It's good enough for me."

" Very well," returned Bartholomew Berg suavely. " And if you decide to place your advertising future in the hands of the Berg, Shriner Company —"

" Now look here," interrupted Ben Griebler again. " I'll tie up with you people when you've shaken something out of your cuffs. I'm not the kind that buys a pig in a poke. We're going to spend money — real money — in this campaign of ours. But I'm not such a come-on as to hand you half a million or so and get a promise in return. I want your plans, and I want 'em in full."

A little exclamation broke from Sam Hupp. He checked it, but not before Berg's curiously penetrating pale blue eyes had glanced up at him, and away again.

" I've told you, Mr. Griebler," went on Bartholomew Berg's patient voice, " just why the thing you insist on is impossible. This firm does not submit advance copy. Every business commission that comes to us is given all the skill, and thought, and enthusiasm, and careful planning that this office is capable of. You know our record. This is a business of ideas. And ideas are too precious, too perishable, to spread in the market place for all to see."

Ben Griebler stood up. His cigar waggled furiously between his lips as he talked.

" I know something else that don't stand

spreading in the market place, Berg. And that's money. It's too darned perishable, too." He pointed a stubby finger at Jock. " Does this fool rule of yours apply to this young fellow, too?"

Bartholomew Berg seemed to grow more patient, more self-contained as the other man's self-control slipped rapidly away.

" It goes for every man and woman in this office, Mr. Griebler. This young chap, McChesney here, might spend weeks and months building up a comprehensive advertising plan for you. He'd spend those weeks studying your business from every possible angle. Perhaps it would be a plan that would require a year of waiting before the actual advertising began to appear. And then you might lose faith in the plan. A waiting game is a hard game to play. Some other man's idea, that promised quicker action, might appeal to you. And when it appeared we'd very likely find our own original idea incorporated in —"

" Say, look here!" squeaked Ben Griebler, his face dully red. " D'you mean to imply that I'd steal your plan! D'you mean to sit there and tell me to my face —"

" Mr. Griebler, I mean that that thing happens constantly in this business. We're almost powerless to stop it. Nothing spreads quicker than a new idea. Compared to it a woman's secret is a sealed book."

Ben Griebler removed the cigar from his lips. He was stuttering with anger. With a mingling of despair and boldness Jock saw the advantage of that stuttering moment and seized on it. He stepped close to the broad table-desk, resting both hands on it and leaning forward slightly in his eagerness.

" Mr. Berg — I have a plan. Mr. Hupp can tell you. It came to me when I first heard that the Grieblers were going to broaden out. It's a real idea. I'm sure of that. I've worked it out in detail. Mr. Hupp himself said it — Why, I've got the actual copy. And it's new. Absolutely. It never —"

" Trot it out! " shouted Ben Griebler. " I'd like to see one idea anyway, around this shop."

" McChesney," said Bartholomew Berg, not raising his voice. His eyes rested on Jock with the steady, penetrating gaze that was peculiar to him. More foolhardy men than Jock McChesney had faltered and paused, abashed, under those eyes. " McChesney, your enthusiasm for your work is causing you to forget one thing that must never be forgotten in this office."

Jock stepped back. His lower lip was caught between his teeth. At the same moment Ben Griebler snatched up his hat from the table, clapped it on his head at an absurd angle and, bristling like a fighting cock, confronted the three men.

" I've got a couple of rules myself," he cried, " and don't you forget it. When you get a little spare time, you look up St. Louis and find out what state it's in. The slogan of that state is my slogan, you bet. If you think I'm going to make you a present of the money that it took my old man fifty years to pile up, then you don't know that Griebler is a German name. Good day, gents."

He stalked to the door. There he turned dramatically and leveled a forefinger at Jock. " They've got you roped and tied. But I think you're a comer. If you change your mind, kid, come and see me."

The door slammed behind him.

"Whew!" whistled Sam Hupp, passing a handkerchief over his bald spot.

Bartholomew Berg reached out with one great capable hand and swept toward him a pile of papers. "Oh, well, you can't blame him. Advertising has been a scream for so long. Griebler doesn't know the difference between advertising, publicity, and bunk. He'll learn. But it'll be an awfully expensive course. Now, Hupp, let's go over this Kalamazoo account. That'll be all, McChesney."

Jock turned without a word. He walked quickly through the outer office, into the great main room. There he stopped at the switch-board.

"Er — Miss Grimes," he said, smiling charmingly. "Where's this Mr. Griebler, of St. Louis, stopping; do you know?"

"Say, where would he stop?" retorted the wise Miss Grimes. "Look at him! The Waldorf, of course."

"Thanks," said Jock, still smiling. And went back to his desk.

At five Jock left the office. Under his arm he carried the flat pasteboard package secured by elastic bands. At five-fifteen he walked

" He made straight for the main desk with its
battalion of clerks "—*Page 119*

swiftly down the famous corridor of the great red stone hotel. The colorful glittering crowd that surged all about him he seemed not to see. He made straight for the main desk with its battalion of clerks.

" Mr. Griebler in? Mr. Ben Griebler, St. Louis? "

The question set in motion the hotel's elaborate system of investigation. At last: " Not in."

" Do you know when he will be in? " That futile question.

" Can't say. He left no word. Do you want to leave your name? "

" N-no. Would he — does he stop at this desk when he comes in? "

He was an unusually urbane hotel clerk. " Why, usually they leave their keys and get their mail from the floor clerk. But Mr. Griebler seems to prefer the main desk."

" I'll — wait," said Jock. And seated in one of the great thronelike chairs, he waited. He sat there, slim and boyish, while the laughing, chattering crowd swept all about him. If you sit long enough in that foyer you will learn all there is to learn about life. An amazing sight

[119]

it is — that crowd. Baraboo helps swell it, and Spokane, and Berlin, and Budapest, and Pekin, and Paris, and Waco, Texas. So varied it is, so cosmopolitan, that if you sit there patiently enough, and watch sharply enough you will even see a chance New Yorker.

From door to desk Jock's eyes swept. The afternoon-tea crowd, in paradise feathers, and furs, and frock coats swam back and forth. He saw it give way to the dinner throng, satin-shod, bejeweled, hurrying through its oysters, swallowing unbelievable numbers of cloudy-amber drinks, and golden-brown drinks, and maroon drinks, then gathering up its furs and rushing theaterwards. He was still sitting there when that crowd, its eight o'clock fresh-ness somewhat sullied, its sparkle a trifle dimmed, swept back for more oysters, more cloudy-amber and golden-brown drinks.

At half-hour intervals, then at hourly intervals, the figure in the great chair stirred, rose, and walked to the desk.

" Has Mr. Griebler come in? "

The supper throng, its laugh a little ribald, its talk a shade high-pitched, drifted towards the street, or was wafted up in elevators. The throng thinned to an occasional group. Then these became rarer and rarer. The revolving door admitted one man, or two, perhaps, who lingered not at all in the unaccustomed quiet of the great glittering lobby.

The figure of the watcher took on a pathetic droop. The eyelids grew leaden. To open them meant an almost superhuman effort. The stare of the new night clerks grew more and more hostile and suspicious. A grayish pallor had settled down on the boy's face. And those lines of the night before stood out for all to see.

In the stillness of the place the big revolving door turned once more, complainingly. For the thousandth time Jock's eyes lifted heavily. Then they flew wide open. The drooping figure straightened electrically. Half a dozen quick steps and Jock stood in the pathway of Ben Griebler who, rather ruffled and untidy, had blown in on the wings of the morning.

He stared a moment. " Well, what —"

" I've been waiting for you here since five o'clock last evening. It will soon be five o'clock again. Will you let me show you those plans now? "

Ben Griebler had surveyed Jock with the

stony calm of the out-of-town visitor who is prepared to show surprise at nothing in New York.

"There's nothing like getting an early start,"
said Ben Griebler. "Come on up to my room."
Key in hand, he made for the elevator. For an
almost imperceptible moment Jock paused.
Then, with a little rush, he followed the short,
thick-set figure. "I knew you had it in you,
McChesney. I said you looked like a comer,
didn't I?"

Jock said nothing. He was silent while
Griebler unlocked his door, turned on the light,
fumbled at the windows and shades, picked up
the telephone receiver. "What'll you have?"

"Nothing." Jock had cleared the center
table and was opening his flat bundle of papers.
He drew up two chairs. "Let's not waste any
time," he said. "I've had a twelve-hour wait
for this." He seemed to control the situation.
Obediently Ben Griebler hung up the receiver,
came over, and took the chair very close to Jock.

"There's nothing artistic about gum," began
Jock McChesney; and his manner was that of a
man who is sure of himself. "It's a shirt-sleeve
product, and it ought to be handled from a shirt-
sleeve standpoint. Every gum concern in the

C. RVB. MONTGOMERY FLAGG

" ' Let's not waste any time,' he said " — *Page 122*

country has spent thousands on a ' better-than-candy ' campaign before it realized that gum is a candy and drug store article, and that no man is going to push a five-cent package of gum at the sacrifice of the sale of an eighty-cent box of candy. But the health note is there, if only you strike it right. Now, here's my idea —"

At six o'clock Ben Griebler, his little shrewd eyes sparkling, his voice more squeakily falsetto than ever, surveyed the youngster before him with a certain awe.

" This — this thing will actually sell our stuff in Europe! No gum concern has ever been able to make the stuff go outside of this country. Why, inside of three years every 'Arry and 'Arriet in England'll be chewing it on bank holidays. I don't know about Germany, but —" He pushed back his chair and got up. " Well, I'm solid on that. And what I say goes. Now I'll tell you what I'll do, kid. I'll take you down to St. Louis with me, at a figure that'll make your —"

Jock looked up.

" Or if you don't want the Berg, Shriner crowd to get wise, I'll fix it this way. I'll go over there this morning and tell 'em I've changed my mind, see? The campaign's theirs, see? Then I refuse to consider any of their suggestions until I see your plan. And when I see it I fall for it like a ton of bricks. Old Berg'll never know. He's so darned high-principled —"

Jock McChesney stood up. The little drawn pinched look which had made his face so queerly old was gone. His eyes were bright. His face was flushed.

" There! You've said it. I didn't realize how raw this deal was until you put it into words for me. I want to thank you. You're right. Bartholomew Berg is so darned high-principled that two muckers like you and me, groveling around in the dirt, can't even see the tips of the heights to which his ideals have soared. Don't stop me. I know I'm talking like a book. But I feel like something that has just been kicked out into the sunshine after having been in jail."

" You're tired," said Ben Griebler. " It's been a strain. Something always snaps after a long tension."

Jock's flat palm came down among the papers with a crack.

"You bet something snaps! It has just snapped inside me." He began quietly to gather up the papers in an orderly little way.

"What's that for?" inquired Griebler, coming forward. "You don't mean —"

"I mean that I'm going to go home and square this thing with a lady you've never met. You and she wouldn't get on if you did. You don't talk the same language. Then I'm going to have a cold bath, and a hot breakfast. And then, Griebler, I'm going to take this stuff to Bartholomew Berg and tell him the whole nasty business. He'll see the humor of it. But I don't know whether he'll fire me, or make me vice-president of the company. Now, if you want to come over and talk to him, fair and square, why come."

"Ten to one he fires you," remarked Griebler, as Jock reached the door.

"There's only one person I know who's game enough to take you up on that. And it's going to take more nerve to face her at six-thirty than it will to tackle a whole battalion of Bartholomew Bergs at nine."

"Well, I guess I can get in a three-hour sleep before — er —"

"Before what?" said Jock McChesney from the door.

Ben Griebler laughed a little shamefaced laugh. "Before I see you at ten, sonny."

V

THE SELF-STARTER

THERE is nothing in the sound of the shrill little bell to warn us of the import of its message. More's the pity. It may be that bore whose telephone conversation begins: " Well, what do you know to-day? " It may be your lawyer to say you've inherited a million. Hence the arrogance of the instrument. It knows its voice will never wilfully go unanswered so long as the element of chance lies concealed within it.

Mrs. Emma McChesney heard the call of her telephone across the hall. Seated in the office of her business partner, T. A. Buck, she was fathoms deep in discussion of the T. A. Buck Featherloom Petticoat Company's new spring line. The buzzer's insistent voice brought her to her feet, even while she frowned at the interruption.

" That'll be Baumgartner 'phoning about

those silk swatches. Back in a minute," said Emma McChesney and hurried across the hall just in time to break the second call.

The perfunctory " Hello ! Yes " was followed by a swift change of countenance, a surprised little cry, then,— in quite another tone — " Oh, it's you, Jock ! I wasn't expecting . . . No, not too busy to talk to you, you young chump ! Go on." A moment of silence, while Mrs. McChesney's face smiled and glowed like a girl's as she listened to the voice of her son. Then suddenly glow and smile faded. She grew tense. Her head, that had been leaning so carelessly on the hand that held the receiver, came up with a jerk. " Jock McChesney ! " she gasped, " you — why, you don't mean ! —"

Now, Emma McChesney was not a woman given to jerky conversations, interspersed with exclamation points. Her poise and balance had become a proverb in the business world. Yet her lips were trembling now. Her eyes were very round and bright. Her face had flushed, then grown white. Her voice shook a little. " Yes, of course I am. Only, I'm so surprised. Yes, I'll be home early. Five-thirty at the latest."

She hung up the receiver with a little fumbling gesture. Her hand dropped to her lap, then came up to her throat a moment, dropped again. She sat staring straight ahead with eyes that saw one thousand miles away.

From his office across the hall T. A. Buck strolled in casually.

"Did Baumgartner say he'd —?" He stopped as Mrs. McChesney looked up at him. A quick step forward —"What's the matter, Emma?"

"Jock — Jock —"

"Jock! What's happened to the boy?" Then, as she still stared at him, her face pitiful, his hand patted her shoulder. "Dear girl, tell me." He bent over her, all solicitude.

"Don't!" said Emma McChesney faintly, and shook off his hand. "Your stenographer can see — What will the office think? Please —"

"Oh, darn the stenographer! What's this bad news of Jock?"

Emma McChesney sat up. She smiled a little nervously and passed her handkerchief across her lips. "I didn't say it was bad, did I? That is, not exactly bad, I suppose."

T. A. Buck ran a frenzied hand over his head. "My dear child," with careful politeness, "will you please try to be sane? I find you sitting at your desk, staring into space, your face white as a ghost's, your whole appearance that of a person who has received a death-blow. And then you say, 'Not exactly bad'!"

"It's this," explained Emma McChesney in a hollow tone: "The Berg, Shriner Advertising Company has appointed Jock manager of their new Western branch. They're opening offices in Chicago in March." Her lower lip quivered. She caught it sharply between her teeth.

For one surprised moment T. A. Buck stared in silence. Then a roar broke from him. "Not exactly bad!" he boomed between laughs. "Not exactly b— Not exactly, eh?" Then he was off again.

Mrs. McChesney surveyed him in hurt and dignified silence. Then —"Well, really, T. A., don't mind me. What you find so exquisitely funny —"

"That's the funniest part of it! That you, of all people, shouldn't see the joke. Not exactly bad!" He wiped his eyes. "Why, do

[132]

you mean to tell me that because your young cub of a son, by a heaven-sent stroke of good fortune, has landed a job that men twice his age would give their eyeteeth to get, I find you sitting at the telephone looking as if he had run off with Annie the cook, or had had a leg cut off!"

"I suppose it is funny. Only, the joke's on me. That's why I can't see it. It means that I'm losing him."

"That's the first selfish word I've ever heard you utter."

"Oh, don't think I'm not happy at his success. Happy! Haven't I hoped for it, and worked for it, and prayed for it! Haven't I saved for it, and skimped for it! How do you think I could have stood those years on the road if I hadn't kept up courage with the thought that it was all for him? Don't I know how narrowly Jock escaped being the wrong kind! I'm his mother, but I'm not quite blind. I know he had the making of a first-class cad. I've seen him start off in the wrong direction a hundred times."

"If he has turned out a success, it's because you've steered him right. I've watched you make him over. And now, when his big chance has come, you —"

" I don't expect you to understand," interrupted Emma McChesney a little wearily. " I know it sounds crazy and unreasonable. There's only one sort of human being who could understand what I mean. That's a woman with a son." She laughed a little shamefacedly. " I'm talking like the chorus of a minor-wail sob song, but it's the truth."

" If you feel like that, Emma, tell him to stay. The boy wouldn't go if he thought it would make you unhappy."

" Not go! " cried Emma McChesney sharply. " I'd like to see him dare to refuse it! "

" Well then, what in —" began Buck, bewildered.

" Don't try to understand it, T. A. It's no use. Don't try to poke your finger into the whirligig they call ' Woman's Sphere.' Its mechanism is too complicated. It's the same quirk that makes women pray for daughters and men for sons. It's the same kink that makes women read the marriage and death notices first in a newspaper. It's the same queer strain that causes a mother to lavish the most love on the weakest, wilfullest child. Perhaps I wouldn't have loved Jock so much if there hadn't been that streak of yellow in him, and if I hadn't had to work so hard to dilute it until now it's only a faint cream color. There ought to be a special prayer for women who are bringing up their sons alone."

Buck stirred a little uneasily. "I've never heard you talk like this before."

"You probably never will again." She swung round to her desk.

T. A. Buck, strolling toward the door, still wore the puzzled look.

"I don't know what makes you take this so seriously. Of course, the boy will be a long way off. But then, you've been separated from him before. What's the difference now?"

"T. A.," said Emma McChesney solemnly, "Jock will be drawing a man-size salary now. Something tells me I'll be a grandmother in another two years. Girls aren't letting men like Jock run around loose. He'll be gobbled up. Just you wait."

"Oh, I don't know," drawled Buck mischievously. "You've just said he's a headstrong young cub. He strikes me as the kind who'd raise the dickens if his three-minute egg happened to be five seconds overtime."

Emma McChesney swung around in her chair. " Look here, T. A. As business partners we've quarreled about everything from silk samples to traveling men, and as friends we've wrangled on every subject from weather to war. I've allowed you to criticise my soul theories, and my new spring hat. But understand that I'm the only living person who has the right to villify my son, Jock McChesney."

The telephone buzzed a punctuation to this period.

" Baumgartner ? " inquired Buck humbly.

She listened a moment, then, over her shoulder, " Baumgartner,"—grimly, her hand covering the mouthpiece —" and if he thinks that he can work off a lot of last year's silk swatches on — Hello! Yes, Mrs. McChesney talking. Look here, Mr. Baumgartner —"

And for the time being Emma McChesney, mother, was relegated to the background, while Emma McChesney, secretary of the T. A. Buck Featherloom Petticoat Company, held the stage.

Having said that she would be home at five-thirty, Mrs. McChesney was home at five-

"He found his mother on the floor . . . surrounded by piles of pajamas, socks, shirts and collars"—*Page 139*

thirty, being that kind of a person. Jock came in at six, breathless, bright-eyed, eager, and late, being that kind of a person.

He found his mother on the floor before the chiffonier in his bedroom, surrounded by piles of pajamas, socks, shirts and collars.

He swooped down upon her from the doorway. "What do you think of your blue-eyed boy! Poor, eh?"

Emma McChesney looked up absently. "Jock, these medium-weights of yours didn't wear at all, and you paid five dollars for them."

"Medium-weights! What in —"

"You've enough silk socks to last you the rest of your natural life. Handkerchiefs, too. But you'll need pajamas."

Jock stooped, gathered up an armful of miscellaneous undergarments and tossed them into an open drawer. Then he shut the drawer with a bang, reached over, grasped his mother firmly under the arms and brought her to her feet with a swing.

"We will now consider the question of summer underwear ended. Would it bore you too much to touch lightly on the subject of your son's future?"

PERSONALITY PLUS

Emma McChesney, tall, straight, handsome, looked up at her son, taller, straighter, handsomer. Then she took him by the coat lapels and hugged him.

"You were so bursting with your own glory that I couldn't resist teasing you. Besides, I had to do something to keep my mind off — off —"

"Why, Blonde dear, you're not —!"

"No, I'm not," gulped Emma McChesney. "Don't flatter yourself, young 'un. Tell me just how it happened. From the beginning." She perched at the side of the bed. Jock, hands in pockets, hair a little rumpled, paced excitedly up and down before her as he talked.

"There wasn't any beginning. That's the stunning part of it. I just landed right into the middle of it with both feet. I knew they had been planning to start a big Western branch. But we all thought they'd pick some big man for it. There are plenty of medium-class dubs to be had. The kind that answers the ad: 'Manager wanted, young man, preferably married, able to furnish A-1 reference.' They're as thick as advertising men in Detroit on Monday morning. But we knew that this

Western branch was going to be given an equal
chance with the New York office. Those big
Western advertisers like to give their money to
Western firms if they can. So we figured that
they'd pick a real top-notcher — even Hopper,
or Hupp, maybe — and start out with a bang.
So when the Old Man called me into his office
this morning I was as unconscious as a babe.
Well, you know Berg. He's as unexpected as
a summer shower and twice as full of electricity.

" ' Morning, McChesney!' he said. ' That
a New York necktie you're wearing?'

" ' Strictly,' says I.

" ' Ever try any Chicago ties?'

" ' Not from choice. That time my suit case
went astray —'

" ' M-m-m-m, yes.' He drummed his fingers
on the table top a couple of times. Then —
' McChesney, what have you learned about advertising in the last two and a half years?'

" I was wise enough as to Bartholomew Berg
to know that he didn't mean any cut-and-dried
knowledge. He didn't mean rules of the game.
He meant tricks.

" ' Well,' I said, ' I've learned to watch a
man's eyes when I'm talking business to him.

If the pupils of his eyes dilate he's listening to you, and thinking about what you're saying. When they contract it means that he's only faking interest, even though he's looking straight at you and wearing a rapt expression. His thoughts are miles away.'

" ' That so ? ' said Berg, and sort of grinned. ' What else ? '

" ' I've learned that one negative argument is worth six positive ones; that it never pays to knock your competitor; that it's wise to fight shy of that joker known as " editorial coöperation." '

" ' That so ? ' said Berg. ' Anything else ? '

" I made up my mind I could play the game as long as he could.

" ' I've learned not to lose my temper when I'm in the middle of a white-hot, impassioned business appeal and the office boy bounces in to say to the boss: " Mrs. Jones is waiting. She says you were going to help her pick out wall paper this morning; " and Jones says, " Tell her I'll be there in five minutes." '

" ' Sure you've learned that ? ' said Berg.

" ' Sure,' says I. ' And I've learned to let the other fellow think your argument's his own.

He likes it. I've learned that the surest kind of copy is the slow, insidious kind, like the Featherloom Petticoat Company's campaign. That was an ideal campaign because it didn't urge and insist that the public buy Featherlooms. It just eased the idea to them. It started by sketching a history of the petticoat, beginning with Eve's fig leaf and working up. Before they knew it they were interested.'

" ' That so? That campaign was your mother's idea, McChesney.' You know, Mother, he thinks you're a wonder."

" So I am," agreed Emma McChesney calmly. " Go on."

" Well, I went on. I told him that I'd learned to stand so that the light wouldn't shine in my client's eyes when I was talking to him. I lost a big order once because the glare from the window irritated the man I was talking to. I told Berg all the tricks I'd learned, and some I hadn't thought of till that minute. Berg put in a word now and then. I thought he was sort of guying me, as he sometimes does — not unkindly, you know, but in that quiet way he has. Finally I stopped for breath, or something, and he said:

PERSONALITY PLUS

" ' Now let me talk a minute, McChesney. Anybody can teach you the essentials of the advertising business, if you've any advertising instinct in you. But it's what you pick up on the side, by your own efforts and out of your own experience, that lifts you out of the scrub class. Now I don't think you're an ideal advertising man by any means, McChesney. You're shy on training and experience, and you've just begun to acquire that golden quality known as balance. I could name a hundred men that are better all-around advertising men than you will ever be. Those men have advertising ability that glows steadily and evenly, like a well-banked fire. But you've got the kind of ability that flares up, dies down, flares up. But every flare is a real blaze that lights things red while it lasts, and sends a new glow through the veins of business. You've got personality, and youth, and enthusiasm, and a precious spark of the real thing known as advertising genius. There's no describing it. You know what I mean. Also, you know enough about actual advertising not to run an ad for a five-thousand-dollar motor car in the " Police Gazette." All of which leads up to this question: How would

you like to buy your neckties in Chicago, Mc-
Chesney?'

" ' Chicago!' I blurted.

" ' We've taken a suite of offices in the new
Lakeview Building on Michigan Avenue.
Would you like your office done in mahogany
or oak?' "

Jock came to a full stop before his mother.
His cheeks were scarlet. Hers were pale. He
was breathing quickly. She was very quiet.
His eyes glowed. So did hers, but the glow
was dimmed by a mist.

" Mahogany's richer, but make it oak, son.
It doesn't show finger-marks so." Then,
quite suddenly, she stood up, shaking a little,
and buried her face in the boy's shoulder.

" Why — why, Mother! Don't! Don't,
Blonde. We'll see each other every few
weeks. I'll be coming to New York to see the
sights, like the rest of the rubes, and I suppose
the noise and lights will confuse me so that I'll
be glad to get back to the sylvan quiet of Chicago. And then you'll run out there, eh?
We'll have regular bats, Mrs. Mack. Dinner
and the theater and supper! Yes?"

"Yes," said Emma McChesney, in muffled tones that totally lacked enthusiasm.

"Chicago's really only a suburb of New York, anyway, these days, and —"

Emma McChesney's head came up sharply. "Look here, son. If you're going to live in Chicago I advise you to cut that suburb talk, and sort of forget New York. Chicago's quite a village, for an inland settlement, even if it has only two or three million people, and a lake as big as all outdoors. That kind of talk won't elect you to the University Club, son."

So they talked, all through supper and during the evening. Rather, Jock talked and his mother listened, interrupting with only an occasional remark when the bubble of the boy's elation seemed to grow too great.

Quite suddenly Jock was silent. After the almost incessant rush of conversation quiet settled down strangely on the two seated there in the living-room with its soft-shaded lamps. Jock picked up a magazine, twirled its pages, put it down, strolled into his own room, and back again.

"Mother," he said suddenly, standing before

her, " there was a time when you were afraid I wasn't going to pan out, wasn't there ? "

" Not exactly afraid, dear, just a little doubtful, perhaps."

Jock smiled a tolerant, forgiving smile. " You see, Mother, you didn't understand, that's all. A woman doesn't. I was all right. A man would have realized that. I don't mean, dear, that you haven't always been wonderful, because you have. But it takes a man to understand a man. When you thought I was going bad on your hands I was just developing, that's all. Remember that time in Chicago, Mother ? "

" Yes," answered Emma McChesney, " I remember."

" Now a man would have understood that that was only kid foolishness. If a fellow's got the stuff in him it'll show up, sooner or later. If I hadn't had it in me I wouldn't be going to Chicago as manager of the Berg, Shriner Western office, would I ? "

" No, dear."

Jock looked at her. In an instant he was all contrition and tenderness. " You're tired.

I've talked you to death, haven't I? Lordy, it's midnight! And I want to get down early to-morrow. Conference with Mr. Berg, and Hupp." He tried not to sound too important.

Emma McChesney took his head between her two hands and kissed him once on the lips, then, standing a-tiptoe, kissed his eyelids with infinite gentleness as you kiss a baby's eyes. Then she brought his cheek up against hers. And so they stood for a moment, silently.

Ten minutes later there came the sound of blithe whistling from Jock's room. Jock always whistled when he went to bed and when he rose. Even these years of living in a New York apartment had not broken him of the habit. It was a cheerful, disconnected whistling, sometimes high and clear, sometimes under the breath, sometimes interspersed with song, and sometimes ceasing altogether at critical moments, say, during shaving, or while bringing the four-in-hand up tight and snug under the collar. It was one of those comfortable little noises that indicate a masculine presence; one of those pleasant, reassuring, man-in-the-house noises that every woman loves.

THE SELF-STARTER

Emma McChesney, putting herself to bed in her room across the hall, found herself listening, brush poised, lips parted, as though to the exquisite strains of celestial music. There came the thump of a shoe on the floor. An interval of quiet. Then another thump. Without having been conscious of it, Emma McChesney had grown to love the noises that accompanied Jock's retiring and rising. His dressing was always signalized by bangings and thumpings. His splashings in the tub were tremendous. His morning plunge could be heard all over the six-room apartment. Mrs. McChesney used to call gayly through the door:

" Mercy, Jock! You sound like a school of whales coming up for air."

" You'll think I'm a school of sharks when it comes to breakfast," Jock would call back. " Tell Annie to make enough toast, Mum. She's the tightest thing with the toast I ever did —"

The rest would be lost in a final surging splash.

The noises in the room across the hall had subsided now. She listened more intently. No, a drawer banged. Another. Then:

" Hasn't my gray suit come back from the tailor's? "

" It was to be sponged, too, you know. He said he'd bring it Wednesday. This is Tuesday."

" Oh! " Another bang. Then: " 'Night, Mother! "

" Good night, dear." Creaking sounds, then a long, comfortable sigh of complete relaxation.

Emma McChesney went on with her brushing. She brushed her hair with the usual number of swift even strokes, from the top of the shining head to the waist. She braided her hair into two plaits, Gretchen fashion. Millions of scanty-locked women would have given all they possessed to look as Emma McChesney looked standing there in kimono and gown. She flicked out the light. Then she, too, relaxed upon her pillow with a little sigh. Quiet fell on the little apartment. The street noises came up to her, now roaring, now growing faint. Emma McChesney lay there sleepless. She lay flat, hands clasped across her breast, her braids spread out on the pillow. In the darkness of the room the years rolled before her in panorama: her girlhood, her marriage, her unhappiness, Jock, the divorce, the struggle for work, those ten years on the road. Those ten years on the road! How she had hated them — and loved them. The stuffy trains, the jarring sleepers, the bare little hotel bedrooms, the bad food, the irregular hours, the loneliness, the hard work, the disappointments, the temptations. Yes but the fascination of it, the dear friends she had made, the great human lesson of it all! And all for Jock. That Jock might have good schools, good clothes, good books, good surroundings, happy times. Why, Jock had been the reason for it all! She had swallowed insult because of Jock. She had borne the drudgery because of Jock. She had resisted temptation, smiled under hardship, worked, fought, saved, succeeded, all because of Jock. And now this pivot about which her whole life had revolved was to be pulled up, wrenched away.

Over Emma McChesney, lying there in the dark, there swept one of those unreasoning night-fears. The fear of living. The fear of life. A straining of the eyeballs in the dark. The pounding of heart-beats.

PERSONALITY PLUS

She sat up in bed. Her hands went to her face. Her cheeks were burning and her eyes smarted. She felt that she must see Jock. At once. Just to be near him. To touch him. To take him in her arms, with his head in the hollow of her breast, as she used to when he was a baby. Why, he had been a baby only yesterday. And now he was a man. Big enough to stand alone, to live alone, to do without her.

Emma McChesney flung aside the covers and sprang out of bed. She thrust her feet in slippers, groped for the kimono at the foot of the bed and tiptoed to the door. She listened. No sound from the other room. She stole across the hall, stopped, listened, gained the door. It was open an inch or more. Just to be near him, to know that he lay there, sleeping! She pushed the door very, very gently. Then she stood in the doorway a moment, scarcely breathing, her head thrust forward, her whole body tense with listening. She could not hear him breathe! She caught her breath again in that unreasoning fear and took a quick step forward.

" Stop or I'll shoot! " said a voice. Simul-

taneously the light flashed on. Emma Mc-
Chesney found herself blinking at a determined
young man who was steadily pointing a short,
chubby, businesslike looking steel affair in her
direction. Then the hand that held the steel
dropped.

" What is this, anyway? " demanded Jock
rather crossly. " A George Cohan comedy? "

Emma McChesney leaned against the foot of
the bed rather weakly.

" What did you think —"

" What would you think if you heard some
one come sneaking along the hall, stopping, listening, sneaking to your door, and then opening
it, and listening again, and sneaking in? What
would you think it was? How did I know you
were going around making social calls at two
o'clock in the morning! "

Suddenly Emma McChesney began to laugh.
She leaned over the footboard and laughed hys-
terically, her head in her arms. Jock stared a
moment in offended disapproval. Then the
humor of it caught him, and he buried his head
in his pillow to stifle unseemly shrieks. His
legs kicked spasmodically beneath the bedclothes.

As suddenly as she had begun to laugh Mrs. McChesney became very sober.

"Stop it, Jock! Tell me, why weren't you sleeping?"

"I don't know," replied Jock, as suddenly solemn. "I — sort of — began to think, and I couldn't sleep."

"What were you thinking of?"

Jock looked down at the bedclothes and traced a pattern with one forefinger on the sheet. Then he looked up.

"Thinking of you."

"Oh!" said Emma McChesney, like a bashful schoolgirl. "Of — me!"

Jock sat up very straight and clasped his hands about his knees. "I got to thinking of what I had said about having made good all alone. That's rot. It isn't so. I was striped with yellow like a stick of lemon candy. If I've got this far, it's all because of you. I've been thinking all along that I was the original electric self-starter, when you've really had to get out and crank me every few miles."

Into Emma McChesney's face there came a wonderful look. It was the sort of look with which a newly-made angel might receive her

[154]

crown and harp. It was the look with which a war-hero sees the medal pinned on his breast. It was the look of one who has come into her Reward. Therefore:

"What nonsense!" said Emma McChesney. "If you hadn't had it in you, it wouldn't have come out."

"It wasn't in me, in the first place," contested Jock stubbornly. "You planted it."

From her stand at the foot of the bed she looked at him, her eyes glowing brighter and brighter with that wonderful look.

"Now see here,"— severely —"I want you to go to sleep. I don't intend to stand here and dispute about your ethical innards at this hour. I'm going to kiss you again."

"Oh, well, if you must," grinned Jock resignedly, and folded her in a bear-hug.

To Emma McChesney it seemed that the next three weeks leaped by, not by days, but in one great bound. And the day came when a little, chattering, animated group clustered about the slim young chap who was fumbling with his tickets, glancing at his watch, signaling a porter for his bags, talking, laughing, trying to hide the pangs of departure under a cloak of gayety and badinage that deceived no one. Least of all did it deceive the two women who stood there. The eyes of the older woman never left his face. The eyes of the younger one seldom were raised to his, but she saw his every expression. Once Emma McChesney's eyes shifted a little so as to include both the girl and the boy in her gaze. Grace Galt in her blue serge and smart blue hat was worth a separate glance.

Sam Hupp was there, T. A. Buck, Hopper, who was to be with him in Chicago for the first few weeks, three or four of the younger men in the office, frankly envious and heartily congratulatory.

They followed him to his train, all laughter and animation.

"If this train doesn't go in two minutes," said Jock, "I'll get scared and chuck the whole business. Funny, but I'm not so keen on going as I was three weeks ago."

His eyes rested on the girl in the blue serge and the smart hat. Emma McChesney saw that. She saw that his eyes still rested there as he stood on the observation platform when the train pulled out. The sight did not pain her as she thought it would. There was success in every line of him as he stood there, hat in hand. There was assurance in every breath of him. His clothes, his skin, his clear eyes, his slim body, all were as they should be. He had made a place in the world. He was to be a builder of ideas. She thought of him, and of the girl in blue serge, and of their children-to-be.

Her breast swelled exultingly. Her head came up.

This was her handiwork. She looked at it, and found that it was good.

" Let's strike for the afternoon and call it a holiday," suggested Buck.

Emma McChesney turned. The train was gone. " T. A., you'll never grow up."

" Never want to. Come on, let's play hooky, Emma."

" Can't. I've a dozen letters to get out, and Miss Loeb wants to show me that new knicker-bocker design of hers."

They drove back to the office almost in silence. Emma McChesney made straight for her desk and began dictating letters with an energy that bordered on fury. At five o'clock she was still working. At five-thirty T. A.

Buck came in to find her still surrounded by papers, samples, models.

"What is this?" he demanded wrathfully, "an all-night session?"

Emma McChesney looked up from her desk. Her face was flushed, her eyes bright, but there was about her an indefinable air of weariness.

"T. A., I'm afraid to go home. I'll rattle around in that empty flat like a hickory nut in a barrel."

"We'll have dinner down-town and go to the theater."

"No use. I'll have to go home sometime."

"Now, Emma," remonstrated Buck, "you'll soon get used to it. Think of all the years you got along without him. You were happy, weren't you?"

"Happy because I had somebody to work for, somebody to plan for, somebody to worry about. When I think of what that flat will be without him — Why, just to wake up and know that you can say good morning to some one who cares! That's worth living for, isn't it?"

"Emma," said T. A. evenly, "do you realize

[158]

" ' Well, you said you wanted somebody to worry about, didn't you?' "— *Page 161*

that you are virtually hounding me into asking you to marry me?"

"T. A.!" gasped Emma McChesney.

"Well, you said you wanted somebody to worry about, didn't you?"

A little whimsical smile lay lightly on his lips.

"Timothy Buck, I'm over forty years old."

"Emma, in another minute I'm going to grow sentimental, and nothing can stop me."

She looked down at her hands. There fell a little silence. Buck stirred, leaned forward. She looked up from the little watch that ticked away at her wrist.

"The minute's up, T. A.," said Emma Mc-Chesney.

THE END

The University of Illinois Press
is a founding member of the
Association of American University Presses.

University of Illinois Press
1325 South Oak Street
Champaign, IL 61820-6903
www.press.uillinois.edu